A Cryptic Christ

A Christmas Spe

Mrs Capper's Casebooks

David W Robinson

In association with Ocelot Press

© David W Robinson 2024
All right reserved

Edited by Maureen Vincent-Northam
Cover Design Rhys Vincent-Northam

No part of this book may be used or reproduced in any manner whatsoever without written permission of the author except for brief quotations used for promotion or in reviews. This is a work of fiction. Names, characters, and incidents are used fictitiously.

Also by David W Robinson

Mrs Capper's Casebooks
Mrs Capper's Christmas
Death at the Wool Fair
Blackmail at the Ballot Box:
Exit Page Ten:
A Professional Dilemma
Murder at Christmas Manor
A Call to Murder
Death of Innocence
Death at the Diet Club
The Christmas Festival Murder
A Quizzical Drowning
Scarborough Not Fair
A Cryptic Christmas Cat-Nabbing
Mrs Capper's Christmas Specials

Prologue

Hello and welcome to Christine Capper's Comings and Goings, your weekly diary of what's been happening in Haxford, brought to you this week by Benny's Bargain Basement, where paying for your Christmas goodies won't leave you with yuletide moodies.

Like most people, I prefer a trouble-free run up to Christmas. I have enough on my plate stringing up decorations, buying food, preparing for the parties, without problems coming from other people, other directions.

And this Christmas would be a mite sadder after daughter Ingrid and her partner, Darren had shot off to the Costa Blanca for the entire winter season. True, we never saw much of them anyway, but they did visit at least once before the big C. This year, they wouldn't. Instead, Dennis and I were planning to fly over there early in the New Year to see them.

Beyond that, having made my TV debut in a short documentary about the goings on at Turpin's Caravan park (where Ingrid and Darren worked during the spring and summer seasons) I was coming under increasing pressure from both TVYK and Radio Haxford to increase my air time.

I resisted. Ignoring the lucrative financial angle, I liked my downtime, and anyway, I felt that one workaholic (Dennis) in our house was enough.

But of course, I wasn't just a middle-aged, wannabe TV and radio celebrity. I was also a private investigator of long standing, and with private eye work, you never knew where or when the next client would come from.

But I knew where it wasn't coming from. Haxford. I'd never been inundated with work, but it became even scarcer through November and into December. It would, I knew, pick up come the New Year. All those illicit liaisons at the office Christmas parties, turning into full blown affairs, leading to angry spouses in need of the evidence. Then the phone would start ringing.

In fact, I was wrong. My next client was imminent, and believe it or not, it was me.

Let me take you back to those cold and dark days in the lead up to the festive season.

Chapter One

Even if I do say so myself, the Christine Capper Interview was one of Radio Haxford's most popular programmes. Going out weekly (or fortnightly when we were short of volunteer interviewees) it was a fast turnaround set up. We could record the interview, which usually took about an hour and a quarter, and our editors could have it cut, primed and ready for broadcast the very next day.

And that had to be the case with the session scheduled for the morning of Thursday December 19, when I chatted with Aidan Compton, assistant general manager of our CutCost branch, who brimmed with avaricious anticipation of the spending spree for the coming party season.

That same degree of expectation burned through me, too, only not so focussed on money. After such an up and down year, the hangover of the accusations laid against me the previous Christmas, suffering the interview with Gil Brophy, plus our chilly (in every sense of the word) visit to Scarborough in October, and losing my (second) precious Renault Clio, I was ready for a total, easy going but sober-ish yuletide.

The fractured arm I picked up in Scarborough healed fairly quickly, which I put down to a sensible diet, lack of tobacco (I'd never smoked) and a moderate intake of alcohol. It was helped by some physio which involved turning and twisting my arm, dipping it in hot wax and squeezing special balls. And before you get the wrong idea, I mean those similar to stress balls, the kind that help you a) relieve tension and b) improve your strength. By the end of November, it was as if nothing had happened to my arm.

The same could not be said for cars. After the Clio was scrapped, Greg Vetch sold Dennis a one-litre Hyundai Amica. One litre was an apt description. It summed up the amount you could safely squeeze into the vehicle. I'm not the largest person in Haxford (honestly, I'm not) but I found that car small and cramped, and when I did the weekly shop, there wasn't enough room in the boot to get everything in. I had to flatten rear seats. Worse, it was an automatic, and habit saw me frequently going for a clutch which didn't exist, and hitting the larger-than-I-was-used-to footbrake pedal instead. In the two weeks I had that car, I carried out more emergency stops than I'd had genuine emergencies in the years since I got my driver's licence.

Dennis had predicted this, and that only aggravated my annoyance. After a frustrating fortnight, I ordered him to find me something else. He whined about the amount he was paying in amendments to our insurance. "They're costing us nearly the same as the cars," he grumbled. But he was a good husband. He did as I asked, sold the car back to Greg (for less than he'd paid for it) and bought me a… Renault Clio. It was dark red, a little older than my last one, but I didn't care. It was like coming home and when he brought it to me, I was especially nice to him that night.

Now, with Christmas not just on the horizon, but

hurtling towards us, I was a happy-ish Radio Haxford interviewer, talking to a feverishly excited store manager.

As always, I had the entire entourage with me during the recording. Eric Reitman, our producer/director, Tom Nixon, our soundman, a couple of techs, and inevitably, Olivia Reitman, Eric's sweet but gormless daughter. As always, she acted as a gofer, and I think Eric only brought her to the interviews because he daren't leave her to her own devices in the studio. If she didn't burn the place down, she'd more than likely sink the whole of Haxford town centre into semi-permanent winter darkness by shorting out the electricity grid.

With so many people in attendance, Aidan's poky little office was way too small, so Aidan cleared a few people from the store's training room, and we settled down for our 80-90-minute chat.

Looking at the world today, we should be used to money grabbers, but I didn't think it would extend to national retail concerns like CutCost. I was wrong, as Aidan's enthusiasm demonstrated.

"Over these final few days," he told me, "we expect to take as much through the checkout as we did in the whole of last month. And don't forget, we're the cheapest in Haxford and the surrounding area. That says something about the way the man in the street will spend money in the run-up to Christmas."

He didn't need to tell me. I was quite familiar with that situation. Even Dennis, whose grip on a pound coin was tighter than many of the wheel nuts he secured on the vehicles Haxford Fixers serviced and repaired, didn't think twice about chucking money around on useless, pointless bits and pieces such as a toy Santa clutching a large spanner, which he and his partners deployed to welcome people to their workshop. Naturally, when it came to buying a Yuletide gift for his loving wife, he searched far and wide to get the lowest possible price.

My spending went through the roof at this time of year, but it was more about necessity than luxury. Feeding Dennis, Cappy the Cat, son Simon and his wife Naomi, and their four-year-old daughter, Bethany (the absolute light of my life) plus all the other people who would turn up at our annual thrash, was not a penny-pinching prospect. Indeed, for all the money I was making from Radio Haxford and the extra I gained from TVYK, Christmas still put a strain on our finances. Worse, sending gifts to Ingrid and her partner Darren was more expensive this year for the simple reason (as I said earlier if you were paying attention) that they floated off to the Costa Blanca.

When I bothered to stop and work it all out, I calculated that we'd be able to visit Ingrid and Darren for about the same price as Christmas was costing us. I didn't tell Dennis that. Squandering money on fripperies was one thing, but if he knew how much the festive season was actually costing, the argument would be long, bitter, and hard fought. I would still be the winner. Of course I would. A threat to stop feeding him would be enough to force him into capitulation, but after such an up-and-down year, I wanted something approaching peace and goodwill over Christmas.

Aidan Compton was of the opposite persuasion. He didn't want a peaceful yuletide. He wanted a supermarket wading in near chaos, a massive battle between customers stripping the shelves and staff trying to refill them to keep up with demand. Halfway through the interview, I began to wonder if Aidan was on some kind of bonus especially when he told us how much more alcohol they would sell. Again, I could readily identify with that. When I bought the Christmas drinks in, I had to have Naomi with me to help me carry it into the house.

Although we recorded an hour or more, the interview was scheduled for only 42 minutes and on broadcast, it would be interrupted for occasional pieces of music and a couple of one-minute news headline slots. Our interview technique was such that on occasion, as signalled by Eric, I would allow a pause between questions or comments. These would allow for the music and news during the one-hour airing.

It goes without saying that the great modern behemoth, the mobile phone had to be switched off or muted when we were interviewing. It was an irritation to younger members of the crew and even some of the interviewees. They were the kind of people who wandered through life with the phone glued to their ear or staring at and working with the screen. Leaving them off, however, was not just a necessity, it was compulsory, and if Eric caught anyone a sneaking a quick glance at their phones during the recording process, they would get the rough edge of his tongue… quietly, of course. We didn't need his anger on the recording any more than we needed the chirrup of a phone.

Which was all very well for these highly paid techs, but I was a private investigator. I couldn't afford to switch it off for fear of missing a potential client. So I muted mine, leaving it in my pocket on vibrate only. At least that way I'd know about missed calls when we were through.

We were about thirty minutes into the recording when I felt the phone vibrate in my pocket. A call? A text message? I didn't know, but that was the idea of the system. It would prompt me to check the phone once we were through.

Needless to say, no one else was aware of it, but about fifteen minutes later, my attention divided between wondering how much longer we had to go, and listening to Aidan's proselytising enthusiasm for CutCost as a company, the Haxford branch in particular, and his interaction with the customers, I noticed Eric remove his headphones, back off several yards, and take out his mobile.

It was unusual and annoying. Eric was a hands-on producer/director. Even in the studio, he didn't wander around the outer office, but sat with the sound men and other technicians, headphones on, keeping a close ear to the output. And annoying? Every time we were out and about, or even when I was broadcasting live for fifteen minutes every Tuesday, during my stint as Radio Haxford's agony aunt, he stressed the need to forget about personal problems, other people, the world in general, and especially mobile phones. And yet, here he was faffing about, reading a text message while we were busy recording.

If I wanted to get technical I did have a problem which could have distracted me. I left home at nine to ensure I was at CutCost for half past so Eric could give us the standard pre-recording briefing, the one which included pushing personal and family issues to the back of our tiny minds. Anyway, at the time I left, Cappy the Cat hadn't come back from his morning ablutions call in the Timmins's garden. It was unusual for him. He didn't like cold weather and normally he was out and back inside five minutes.

I wasn't worried. It wasn't the first time it had happened, and it was possible that there was a new she-cat on the block. The biggest stumbling block would be getting him out of his bad mood when I got home. Not for nothing did I often refer to him as our petulant pussy.

Eric's message obviously had nothing to do with missing moggies. Whatever the content of the text, I could see the puzzlement in his face. Beryl, I wondered? The thought only annoyed me further. If I had a text message from Dennis (so remote that the sun would probably die before it happened) he would come down on me from a great height. Eric, I mean, not Dennis. The rule was absolute, rigid, and there were no exceptions. Correction: there was one exception which proved the rule. Eric, I'm in charge and you'll do as I say not as I do, Reitman.

When the actual interview was over, Aidan rang through to the store's cafeteria and ordered tea and coffee and snacks all round, and then sat back to watch as we dealt with the introduction and the au revoir, plus a couple of music and news cues. It was standard form. I always recorded these after the interview. Once they were done to Eric's demanding standards, Tom and his guys began to dismantle their equipment.

A general buzz of conversation began to fill the room, Aidan exchanging views with our crew on what they would be doing over Christmas, and after helping myself to a cup of tea and a chocolate digestive biscuit (CutCost own brand, not my preferred McVities) I collared Eric and asked, "What was so disturbing about that message you received?"

He chuckled. "That obvious, was it?"

"It called to mind the number of times you've told me to keep my phone out of the way when we're recording."

"Yes. Of course. It was just that for me to receive a text message is so unusual that I thought it might be a family emergency. Schools are out for the Christmas break, Beryl's home alone, and for a moment I was worried that she'd fallen ill or something. Absolutely no reason for me to believe that. You know her. She's never ill."

I didn't know her that well. I mean, for all I knew, she might come down with PMS every fortnight rather than once a month. But I wasn't disposed to argue. "Yes. Right. But you're always warning us about phones, and—"

He cut me off. "In fact, the message came from the studio, and they were forwarding a text they've received for you."

"For me?" Smacked in the gob I have never been so. "Anyone who wants to send me a text message can send it to my number. They don't have to text Radio Haxford."

"True, but it happens more than you may imagine, Chrissy. We get any number of messages for you. True, many listeners actually phone in, but we still get our share of text messages and emails, most of them praising you. This one was different which is why the station forwarded it to me. Quite frankly, it's gobbledygook." Eric took out his phone, accessed the message, and passed it to me.

He was right. It was total nonsense.

FAO Christine Capper. Hello catch nipper sire, for catch pet pay let's say an even five. Viz failed Dan.

Aidan crossed the floor, carrying fresh coffee for both of us. "Nothing wrong, is there?"

"Trolls," I declared. "Sending nonsense messages via text."

Eric showed him the message, and Aidan came to a surprising conclusion. "To be honest, it's packed with what look like anagrams. It looks like a complicated, cryptic crossword clue. Are you into crosswords, Christine?"

I shrugged. "Simple ones, yes. Like the fifteen minute coffee time crosswords you find in some newspapers and magazines, but I don't tackle things like The Times or The Telegraph."

It was perfectly true. I had tried them in the past, but the key to cryptic crosswords was trying to get a clue to the way the compiler was thinking. I recalled Dennis's opinion on the matter.

"Who's got the time for craptic crisswords? Engines are simpler."

To Dennis, maybe, but to me engines were just as complicated as tough crosswords.

Focusing on Aidan, I said, "If that's what it looks like to you, what does it mean?"

He shook his head. "Haven't a clue. I mean, I do this kind of crossword, but you've got to have some kind of a hint as to the way the setter is thinking." (Didn't I just say so?) "There's absolutely no logic about this, and it would take an awful lot of thinking about to come to any conclusion. Is this the first one you've received?"

"This came to the Radio Haxford studio. I've never received one at all." That very statement reminded me that my phone had vibrated during the recording. I took it from my pocket, unlocked the screen, and sure enough, there was a text alert. I opened it, and found exactly the same message the studio had received.

"What on earth is this?"

It was a rhetorical question, but Aidan decided to answer it anyway. "Somebody taking the mick with you, Christine. We get this kind of twaddle all the time. Not as complicated as this, of course, but we do get people bombarding us with text messages complaining about anything and everything, from cold coffee in the cafeteria, to the price of fresh apples which aren't fresh enough."

"Having bought some of those apples, I can understand it, Aidan. And no, that's not a criticism. It was just one pack I bought which were too close to their sell by date."

"You should have brought them back. You know our policy. We'd have exchanged them."

"If we could stick to the subject," Eric intervened. "This kind of thing can be seen as a nuisance, perhaps even malicious, and if we want to get technical about it, Chrissy, you could report it, I'm sure Mandy Hiscoe would listen to you."

"She might, but only after she's thrown a hissy fit," I said. "We're in the run-up to Christmas, Eric, and Mandy, Simon, and all the rest of the police, will be running round like blue…" I only just caught myself before finishing the familiar idiom. "Idiots," I corrected myself. "What they don't need is me complaining about morons sending incomprehensible messages." I chewed my lip for a moment. "I'll have a word with my daughter-in-law when I get home. Naomi's quite clever with this kind of crossword." I checked my watch. Coming up to eleven o'clock. "For now, if no one's any objections, I'd like to grab a trolley and get round the shop to do my buying. I'll see you on Tuesday for the agony aunt slot. That's if I don't see you before."

I moved back to the table where we had carried out the recording, and picked up my coat. As I put it on, Olivia came to my side.

"Did I hear right, Mrs Dapper. Someone's sending you crappy sex messages?"

She was a lovely girl. About twenty-four years of age, very pretty, sweet, good natured, she didn't have one evil bone in her slender body, but when it came to brains, she must have been in the back of the queue when they were handing them out. Getting my name wrong was consistent, interpreting cryptic text messages as crappy sex messages was entirely in keeping with her customary lack of intelligence. You could tell her anything, and if she were to repeat it seconds later, it would bear little resemblance to what you had said.

"Don't you worry about it, Olivia. It's just nonsense."

"You have to watch them, Pristine. And it's ill-wossname. Legal. You can retort it to the police." She smiled. "But you already know that, don't you. You used to be Napper the Copper, didn't you?"

I had a lot to get through, so it was simpler to agree with her. "Yes, love, I did. Now you do know that you're invited to our house on Boxing Day, don't you?"

"I'm looking forward to it. Will there be plenty of gorgeous young men there?" She cast an anxious glanced back at her father. "Don't tell Dad I asked that, will you?"

I couldn't help chuckling. How naive could any girl of her age be? "It'll be our little secret, Olivia. I'll see on Tuesday morning for the agony aunt spot."

Chapter Two

With several hundredweight of Christmas shopping to be gathered, paid for, and carried home (in my car, obviously) the last thing I needed was a distraction in the shape of an internet/text troll, but as I made my slow way round the shop, dithering between CutCost own brand mince pies and top priced, well-known alternatives, I couldn't put it out of my mind.

It was those six words, *pay let's say an even five*. Pay? For what? And what did an even five mean? Five pounds? Five hundred? Five thousand? Five pounds of potatoes?

And why me? What had I done to deserve the unwanted attention of some barmpot who probably had too much time on his hands and too many fantasies to indulge, or too many scams to run? And yes, I had good reason to believe it came from a man, because they usually did.

I was well-known in the Haxford/Huddersfield area, thanks primarily to my blog/vlog, enhanced over the last couple of years by my air time on Radio Haxford and latterly, TVYK, not to mention some of my more nationally reported efforts as a private investigator.

I was active on a number of social media channels, and beyond the West Yorkshire boundaries, I had a small following which spread across the world, would you believe? Well, frankly, it doesn't matter whether you believe it or not, it's true. That being the case, it was inevitable that I had some contact from scammers and spammers. They were easy to recognise despite their sometimes absurd efforts to cover up their nefarious activities, and I ignored them. In more persistent instances, I blocked them.

But such was the state of social media that it was impossible to catch them all and with the advent of smartphones the problem had become worse. No matter how you tried to hide it, there were ways and means of discovering your number. In my case, it wasn't difficult because as a private investigator, I had to make my number public. How else would clients contact me?

Haxford Fixers, Dennis's outfit, also had an active social media presence. As a relatively successful business, it was incumbent upon them to do so, but at those the times I'd checked the news feeds, it was usually Lester Grimes promising all and sundry a good time at the Sump Hole (Haxford's nickname for the Engine House pub). Dennis probably got his share of spam from alleged East European women offering him a 'good time'. Not that he would ever be interested. East European women tended not to own classic British cars.

This particular text message was out of left field as our American friends would say. What does that mean? Haxford is situated in a moorland area, and we have fields left right and centre, and if someone is throwing mud and stones at you, whether for sheer spite or because you've driven too fast and panicked their flock of sheep, they can come from either side.

I'm digressing. This message was strange

because it was so complicated and nonsensical, and yet I had the feeling that it meant something. Perhaps someone fancied me. A fantasist who had seen me on TV or in the local newspapers, and decided that he'd like to sleep with me. That was a euphemism, by the way. Sleeping was the last thing on the warped minds of these sad people.

Again, I had to ask why me? I considered myself a good-looking woman, but I was hardly a stud (yuk) magnet (yuk, yuk). True, I was a bit broader in the beam these days, but what would anyone expect from a woman in her early fifties? Dennis still found me alluring. Not often, but when the mood took him… On reflection that wasn't the best recommendation. Dennis found his 1979 Morris Marina glamorous, but to me it was a pile of clapped out, uncomfortable junk. He was in love with the old wrecker Haxford Fixers used, a huge, monstrous, and ungainly lorry. There were no other women in his life, other than his mother and Sandra Limpkin who ran the Snacky on the third floor of Haxford Mill, and the only thing he loved about Sandra was the food she served. Besides, she weighed in at a good few stones above me, so perhaps it wasn't surprising that he still found me eye-catching.

Putting Dennis aside, I could still turn a few heads, but they tended to turn slower these days, thanks to problems like arthritis, a common complaint amongst the age of the men I'm talking about.

Having said all that, I was not and never had been the stuff of male fantasies. I never did have an hourglass figure, I never had a serious cleavage to show off, and if my lower legs could be described as strong, even chunky, what would you expect from a former police officer who had spent years tramping the streets of Haxford to keep the rowdies under control?

So again the question posed itself. Why me?

Hovering around the confectionary aisle, asking myself should it be Quality Street, Roses or both, trying to make up my mind which flavour Pringles I should take, I decided I would abandon the text message problem for the time being and get on with my shopping. And yet, as I elected to take both boxes of chocolates, plus a box of Heroes, two packs of After Eight Mints, and one of each of the multitude of Pringle flavours, the problem came back to me and with it, a potential solution. Hadn't I already mentioned Haxford Fixers and Lester 'Grimy' Grimes?

Lester was the junior partner Haxford Fixers, the electrical specialist, and throughout the years I'd known him (well over a decade) he'd always employed this cheeky, insouciant, and suggestive approach towards me. How many times had I called at the workshop only to be greeted by Lester saying, "Hey up, it's cuddly Chrissy. Looking for a wild night with an old raver like me, are you darlin'?"

True, it never went further than cheeky remarks, but as I made my way along the frozen food aisle, dropping two large bags of oven chips into my trolley, I wondered whether he had begun to take the matter more seriously, or with his sense of humour – always naughty, always questionable – it had taken a more twisted turn.

Adding two bags of frozen chicken wings and thighs to the mass in the trolley, I dismissed the idea right away. Lester might well harbour designs upon me (not that they would ever get him anywhere) but I doubted that he had the intelligence to put together such a complicated, cryptic message.

I don't know how long it took me to get through the checkout. I was in the queue for a good ten minutes, and I swear it took the same time, possibly longer, for the operator to scan my purchases, then present me with a demand for payment that reminded me of the last quarter's gas and electricity bill.

At length, however, I wheeled my trolley out into the car park, unlocked my new (to me) Clio, opened the boot, and as I began to stack the carrier bags, all ten of them, into the car, I noticed a small clutch of police vehicles on the far side of the car park, about a hundred and fifty yards from me and alongside them were two readily recognisable plainclothes officers. My son, Detective Constable Simon Capper, and his immediate superior, Detective Sergeant Mandy Hiscoe, and they appeared to be waiting for someone getting out of a patrol car.

I've always said that nosy goes with the lot of a private investigator, and once I had my car loaded, I locked it up again, gathered my topcoat about myself to fend off the bitter cold, and walked over to them.

"We've nowt to say, Mam," Simon greeted me, and Mandy supported him.

"You can read about the court case if and when it happens, Chrissy," she said.

I tutted. "You two really are the pits. Here I am, your loving mother, Simon, one of your best friends, Mandy, and you won't even share gossip with me. I mean, it's not like I'm a news reporter, is it?"

"All I'll say, Chrissy, is, it's iffy," Mandy said. "I'm telling you no more than that."

And that moment Constable Sonny Scott climbed out of the patrol car and ambled across to join us. He spoke directly to Mandy. "Sorry, Sarge, but Aubrey is insisting that it's nonsense, and if you want him down the station, we'll have to arrest him. But he's kicking off. He says it never happened."

Mandy tutted and gave Sonny a silent dressing down with a stare that matched the icy weather. "Arrest him on suspicion, and get him down to the station. I'll follow you." She turned on me. "One word about this anywhere, Chrissy, and you're knee deep in it."

"I've told you before, Mandy, I'm not in news. And you should know me better. I won't say a word until I hear some kind of official announcement. Listen, while I'm here, can I just put a teeny-weeny problem to Simon?"

My son laughed. "You're always a problem, Mam."

"A crime?" Mandy asked.

"Nuisance communication," I told her, "but it's strange, and I just want to know if you've seen anything like it."

Mandy gave permission with a nod, and Simon

and I stepped off to one side. I took out my phone, opened the bizarre text message, and showed it to him.

He must have read it two or three times before he finally announced, "It's garbage. Before you ask, no, I've never seen anything like this. And to my knowledge, we haven't had any reports of this kind of rubbish."

I took the phone back. "It's those half-dozen words, Simon. Pay, let's say, an even five. I'm worried that I could get more of this rubbish, so I could do with working out what it all means. According to Aidan Compton, it reads like a complicated crossword clue."

His eyes lit. "There you are, then. Get on the horn to Nam. She does those kind of crosswords for fun."

"Really?" I was being coy. Hadn't I told Aidan that Naomi liked this kind of crossword? That thought prompted another. "Her name is Naomi."

"She prefers Nam. Beth's finished school for the Christmas holidays, and Nam'll be sitting round the house twiddling her thumbs. Are you on your way home?"

"Yes I am, and your daughter's name is Bethany."

He ignored my remonstrations. "When you get home, give Nam a shout, and I'm sure she'll come down with Beth, and she'll sort the message for you, see if she can make any sense of it." As he spoke, he stressed the words 'Nam' and 'Beth'.

"I'll do that. Oh, while I think on, if Sonny was talking about Harold Aubrey, a lawyer, you do know that he's a… Well, not exactly a friend, but certainly an associate of your Uncle Stephen." Stephen Fordice was my younger brother, and one of Haxford's top solicitors.

"Makes no difference to us, Mam, but I'll mention it to Mandy. Not that Aubrey's likely to call Stephen. He's perfectly capable of defending himself."

"I suppose so. Now don't forget, you, Naomi, and Bethany, are expected on Christmas Day, and again on Boxing Day." This time I stressed the words 'Naomi' and 'Bethany'.

He didn't react other than to say, "If I can get the time off."

I stretched up, pecked him on the cheek, gave Mandy a wave, and then made my way back to my car.

Settling behind the wheel, I ran the engine, waiting for the heaters to warm up. This was my third Clio, and although I was no expert on cars (that was Dennis's forte) the one thing I could say in favour of the Clio was that the heaters were fantastic. They warmed up in next to no time. Even running *down* the steep hill from our house into Haxford, the heaters would be working effectively within half a mile of leaving home. Sitting on the CutCost car park, leaving the engine to idle, it would take a good few minutes, and I passed the time by ringing Naomi, and inviting her to lunch.

She agreed, and after a bit of a natter, I fastened my seatbelt, slotted the car into gear, let the handbrake off, and drove sedately out of the car park, to the traffic lights, where I turned right towards Haxford town centre, and beyond it, home.

It was about quarter to twelve when I parked in the drive. There was no sign of Cappy the Cat, and it caused me to wonder precisely where he would be sulking. My next-door neighbour Hazel McQuarrie often took him in for us, but that was when we were away on holiday, not because he'd managed to get himself locked out.

I was in the middle of moving the shopping from the car to the kitchen when Naomi's tidy little Toyota pulled into the drive and nosed up to my car.

Naomi Capper was the daughter I wanted Ingrid to be. Pretty, vivacious, outgoing, a bit of a party animal, but a woman for whom family came first, and by family, I didn't just mean Simon and daughter, Bethany. Naomi took just as much interest in Dennis and me as she did her husband and daughter. I'd go so far as say she took more interest in us than she did her own family, but that could well be because she was a Mancunian by birth. She met Simon when they were at University together, and when they eventually decided to marry, she moved to Haxford. If anyone wanted my opinion, Haxford was infinitely preferable to Manchester anyway.

She let Bethany out of the rear child seat, and this tiny light of my life hurtled towards me and threw herself into my arms, crying, "Nanna."

I spent a moment hugging her, then put her down, carried on with the job of moving the shopping to the kitchen, this time with Naomi's help.

Five minutes later, a mass of groceries piled on

the kitchen floor, we settled at the kitchen table, waiting for the kettle to boil, and listening to Bethany's adventures on the previous day's end of school (which she pronounced schoo-wul) term.

"We had a chris (large intake of breath) muss play, and I was a shep (large intake of breath) herd, and then we sang Christmas car (large intake of breath) ols."

"And I'll bet yours was the sweetest voice in school," I said.

"It was. Did you sing for chris (large intake of breath) muss when you were at schoo-wul?"

"It was so long ago, darling, I really can't remember."

She settled, playing with a child's tablet, while Naomi and I set about putting the shopping away, after which I made tea for the both of us, supplied Bethany with a soft drink, and we sat at the table again.

"I bumped into Simon on the car park at CutCost. He was attending some kind of incident. I can't tell you any more than that, Naomi, because he wouldn't tell me anything. But he did tell me to speak to you about a complicated text message I've received."

I took up my phone, opened the message, laid the phone on the table, and turned it towards her.

"Phew. That's a bit of a stinker." She gulped down a mouthful of tea, and frowned at the message. "I deal with this kind of thing in crosswords, Chrissy, but it's easier when you have a few letters in place. With this, you've got absolutely nothing. Really, I need to break it down into separate phrases to see if I can make sense of it, but there's no punctuation to give us an idea of the different phrases. I mean, the way it begins, 'hello catch nipper sire' could almost be a greeting, but as to who... Oh, hang on. I just wonder..."

She trailed off, and I could see which way her mind was working. I left the table, scrabbled in a drawer, came out with a notebook and pen, and passed it to her.

Her technique made sense. She wrote out the entire line first. *Hello catch nipper sire, for catch pet pay let's say an even five. Viz failed Dan.* Underneath that, she wrote the first four words in capital letters, and then she began to strike them out and write below them. C-H-R-I...

Long before she finished, I guessed where she was going.

She turned the pad towards me. "It's definite. Those opening words translate as, 'Hello, Christine Capper'." Her eyes burned into me. "Whoever this nutter is, he's talking directly to you."

I didn't feel particularly alarmed. "A bit obvious, really, Naomi, considering he sent it not only to my phone, but also to Radio Haxford where it was marked, FAO Christine Capper. So he's talking to me, but what is he saying?"

She chuckled. "Happen he fancies a roll on the rug with you." She became more serious. "The rest of it'll take some working out, but if I'm right, it's called sexting, and you'd be better checking with Simon, but I'm sure it's an offence. Malicious communication." She cast a wary eye on her daughter, to ensure that she wasn't listening, but

Bethany was totally engrossed in whatever she was doing on her tablet. All the same, Naomi lowered her voice. "It could even be sexual harassment."

"It won't get him anywhere," I said. "Other than a good kick where he wouldn't want to show his mother. Would you care to work on it while I put lunch together?"

"Sure. It's better than sitting around the house twiddling my thumbs trying to find something to watch on today's god-awful TV."

"Sandwiches okay?"

She nodded and while she bowed her head over the message and notepad, I moved to the worktops and began to prepare a light lunch for the three of us.

Bethany was easily dealt with. A pack of McCain's Microchips (or whatever they called them these days) had her settled. For Naomi and myself, I opened a small can of corned beef, and put together two sandwiches each, and then prepared fresh tea.

About a quarter of an hour later, I set everything on the table, sat opposite Naomi once more, and while we ate, I looked to her for some answers.

"It's difficult, Chrissy. I haven't a clue with those three words, viz failed Dan, but before that, it reads, 'for catch pet pay let's say an even five' and although it sounds like a demand for money it doesn't say what for."

"Nor exactly how much. An even five. I mean, five isn't even an even number." I had to pause and think for a minute about the number of times I'd use the word 'even' in that last sentence.

I glanced around the room, as if seeking

inspiration, and my eyes fell upon Cappy the Cat's food and water dishes. "Where on earth is that antisocial animal got to?"

At that point Bethany looked up. "I haven't see (large intake of breath) n Kitty the c (large intake of breath) at, Nanna."

"No, darling, neither have I."

I noticed that Naomi's attention was suddenly focused on the puzzle. Her eyes lit, then gaped. "Oh my God."

"What?" I was filled with anxiety. "What is it?"

"He's mentioned. In this sentence. Catch pet pay. It's not a demand for money, Chrissy. It's an anagram of Cappy the Cat. Ignoring this viz failed Dan, the message actually reads, hello, Christine Capper. For Cappy the Cat, let's say an even five." She stared up at me. "It sounds to me like someone's kidnapped your bad-tempered moggie."

Chapter Three

"What?" As I asked the question, I laughed, a sort of 'I can't believe that' laugh. You know the kind of thing I mean. "Who on earth would want to kidnap that ratty ragamuffin?"

One look at Naomi's face told me she was deadly serious. "I'm sorry, Chrissy, but that's the way I interpret it. Course, I could be wrong."

Alongside her, Bethany had suddenly lost interest in her tablet and was paying close attention to our discussion. "Nanna, has ca (large intake of breath) ` the cap gone to sl (large intake of breath) eep. Only when Mam has a sleep (large intake of breath) she calls it an (large intake of breath) ap."

"It's a bit more complicated than that, chicken," Naomi said. "But don't you worry about it. Nanna and I will sort it out." My daughter-in-law swung back to me. "Like I say, I could be wrong, but that's the way I read it. You need an expert on cryptic crosswords or anagrams, or whatever. I'm not an expert. I'm just a groupie."

I shook my head. "No. I don't believe it. And I can do better than an expert. Can you hang on five minutes while just nip next door to see Mrs McQuarrie?"

She gave me a shrug and a nod of agreement, and without bothering to pick up a coat, I hurried out into the icy weather, rushed next door, rang the bell, and as I pushed the door open I called out, "Hazel? It's Chrissy from next door."

"Come on in, lass," she invited from the front

room.

I made my way into find the place in its usual state of disarray, but made worse by a large, half-packed suitcase.

"Leaving town, Hazel?" I asked.

"Too right. Bobby and I are shooting off to Tenerife first thing tomorrow morning."

This came as a surprise. "You're going to miss Christmas?"

"No. His family are coming with us, we'll have a proper knees up in Playa de Las Américas."

I was impressed. At her age, I thought jet-setting would be a thing of the past, although you'd be hard pressed to describe southern Tenerife as jet-setting. "I don't know how you can do that," I said. "I love Christmas at home, here with the family."

"And I suppose you love the ice, snow, the cold nights, the short days? Not for me, girl. Forecast for the Canaries is wall-to-wall sunshine and daytime temperatures up around twenty-five degrees." She sat down in an armchair, obviously in need of a breather. "Anyway, was there something you wanted?"

Her packing and her holiday plans had forced Cappy the Cat to the back of my mind. "Oh, yes, sorry, Hazel. Have you seen anything of Cappy today? My cat. Only I had to go out this morning. I had an interview to record, and he wasn't back when I left. I haven't seen him since. I just wondered whether he'd come to you to get in out of the cold."

Her lips pursed. "I'm sorry, Chrissy, but no. I haven't seen him. And I know how much he likes staying with me when you're on holiday."

That was pure nonsense. Cappy the Cat hated it when we left him with Hazel. With her, he had to do as he was told, and not as he pleased. Obviously, he never took it out on her. He waited until we got back, and vented his frustration on us.

"Have you tried Archie Prenton?"

"The vet?"

She nodded. "I'm just thinking if someone found him wandering about in the cold, thought he was a stray, they might have picked him up and taken him to Prenton's place. Other than that, there's always Bertha Ginsburgh's cattery on Huddersfield Road."

It didn't sound likely. Archie Prenton had no more love for Cappy the Cat than Cappy the Cat had for Archie Prenton, and when it was necessary to take him for treatment, it was always a toss-up who came off the worst. Cappy the Cat wearing a cone of shame, or Archie Prenton nursing the claw marks on the back of his hands.

"I'll give them both a call. I'd better shoot off, Hazel, let you get on. If I don't see you before, have a nice time in Tenerife."

"Sunshine, sea, gallons of cheap booze, and sharing a bed with a man of my dreams, what could be better?"

Her last announcement made me smile. Hazel McQuarrie was coming up to her eightieth birthday, and I had an idea that 'the man of her dreams' Bobby Emburey was a year or two older than her. If they were sharing a bed together, it would be to sleep and nothing more exciting. Even so, I hoped I still had her zest for life when I got to her age.

Eager to get out of the cold, I hurried back into our kitchen where Naomi greeted me expectantly. "Well?"

"Mrs Mcq hasn't seen him. Give me a minute, and I'll ring the vet. See if anyone's dropped him off there."

Archibald Prenton MRCVS, was the only practising vet in Haxford. That always came as something of a surprise to me considering the town's location in the middle of moors scattered with cattle and sheep, but most of the surrounding farmers seemed to prefer vets from Huddersfield. Understandable when you were aware of Prenton's grumpy approach to the job.

Aged about fifty, chunky, a red, jowly face someone once described as similar to potatoes mashed in tomato sauce, he rarely smiled, and where Cappy the Cat was concerned, it wasn't just rare, it was never.

Oddly enough, he answered the phone rather than his receptionist or nurse or whatever she was.

"It's Christine Capper, Mr Prenton. My cat, Cappy, is missing. I'm wondering whether anyone picked him up thinking he was a stray, and brought him to you to keep him out of the cold."

"I have enough on my plate, Mrs Capper, without taking in evil strays like that vicious little feline of yours."

"You don't appear to worry about it when you're taking the money out of my purse, Mr Prenton." I know, I know. I should learn when to shut my mouth but his response irritated me to the point where I couldn't keep quiet. "Putting aside our personal differences, have you seen my cat today?"

"No, madam, I have not, and in case I haven't made myself clear, I wouldn't worry if I never saw him again."

"In that case, Mr Prenton I'll bid you good day. I might have been tempted to wish you all the best for Christmas, but I doubt that Cappy the Cat would echo my sentiments."

I cut the call before he could give me any further vitriol.

I wandered back into the kitchen, pondering where that stupid cat could have got to. Barbara Timmins was a possibility. No, she was not. Our moody little moggy insisted upon using her back garden as a public convenience, and if she saw him out in the cold, she'd more than likely throw ice cubes at him in an effort to freeze him to death. She'd then probably nail him to a plaque and put it up on the wall as a warning to other feral felines which might be tempted to abuse her back lawn.

My only remaining option was, as Hazel McQuarrie suggested, Bertha Ginsburgh. She was something of an institution in Haxford. Come to that, she was built like an institution. Large, bulky, and ungainly. I couldn't doubt her sincerity or her love of cats, but when it came to the owners, her attitude was little short of pugnacious. Still, with most other avenues leading nowhere, I had no choice, and I dug out her number and rang.

After several rings, it cut to an answerphone, and Bertha's thick voice announced, "I'm out. Leave a message."

It wasn't only the brevity of the message, but the

acid tones in which it was delivered which got to me. It was less a polite request, more of an order. But that was Bertha all over. She was, I think, somewhere in her 60s, although I could be wrong about that. I don't know that she was ever married, but it would take a man of superhuman heroism to handcuff himself to her.

I decided against leaving a message. I had other ideas regarding this absurd text, and Cappy the Cat would no doubt turn up in his own time, chock-a-bloc with a similar attitude to Bertha's.

I returned to the kitchen where Naomi was busy washing up the few dishes.

"We're going to get off home, Chrissy. You really need to get someone to look at this text, just in case I'm right."

"I'll give Ian at the Recorder a bell. He uses freelancers to compile the paper's crosswords."

"And what about Cappy the Cat? Suppose he really has been bagged?"

I shook my head. "I can't see it. You know how vicious he can be. Anyone trying to pick him up would be risking their eyesight, even their eyes. I'll let you know."

We spent a few minutes getting Bethany into her coat and gloves, and then they left me, at which point, I made myself a fresh cup of tea, took myself in to one of the small settees in the conservatory, huddling up to the radiator, and rang the Recorder.

They knew me well enough to put me straight through to Ian Noiland, the managing editor, and he greeted me cheerily. "Afternoon, Chrissy. Looking to run a few adverts with us?"

"At your prices, not this side of hell freezing over. No, fact is, Ian, I have a bit of a problem. I've received a bizarre text message this morning, and just had a word with my daughter-in-law, and she thinks it's a threat. She suggested I get an expert on cryptic crosswords to look at it, and right away, I thought of you and your freelancers."

He hummed and aahed for a moment. "Toughie, is it?"

"Definitely. I don't do that kind of crossword so I don't really have a clue. Can you help?"

"I think we may be able to. We have this cryptic genius on our books. Norman Rushcroft. Do you know him?"

"It doesn't ring any bells. A local, is he?"

"He lives between here in Huddersfield. I can give him a bell, ask him to come on down and if you can get yourself down here too, bring the message with you, and I'm certain he'll give it a good coat of thinking about." He paused for less than a second. "While you're on the phone, what do you know about Harold Aubrey?"

"Nothing," I said. "All right, I know he's a lawyer, and I was in CutCost this morning when he was arrested. I don't know what he's supposed to have done."

He chuckled. "Come on, Chrissy. You're just being tight-lipped."

"No, Ian, seriously. Mandy Hiscoe was there and our Simon, but they wouldn't tell me anything. What is he supposed to have done, d'you know?"

"I just asked you that."

"Well, I'm sorry, but I can help you. But as

always, if I hear anything... I won't say a word to you." I glanced at the clock. "I'll be with you in, what? Twenty minutes?"

"I'll have coffee ready."

Having made the arrangement, I gulped down the coffee, opened the conservatory door, called out to Cappy the Cat a few times, and when he didn't show, I locked up, put on my winter woollies again, made my way out to the car, and minutes later, I was on my way back down to Haxford.

Even now, I did not accept Naomi's analysis of the message. It was all right for her saying that it mentioned Cappy the Cat, but how many people would know that we called our miserable moggie by that name?

As I made the intersection with the southern bypass, it occurred to me that most of Haxford, possibly West Yorkshire, maybe half the country, would know my cat's name. I mentioned him frequently in my vlogs and blogs, he rated more than the occasional mention on my website, and my social media pages carry plenty of photographs of him.

That didn't mean Naomi had it right, but as I made my way through the intersection and up to the market hall parking area, the first hint of worry crossed my mind, and with it a good dose of annoyance. If anyone had hurt my pet, they would pay for it. Whatever damage Cappy the Cat didn't do, I'd make up for. No one attacked the Capper family like that.

From the car park to the Recorder offices was a walk of about 200 yards, and as I made my way there, my phone bleated for attention, but it was an incoming call, not a text message, and as with so many of my callers, it was an unrecognised number.

Sheltering from the vicious wind by huddling into a corner by the entrance to the market hall, I answered the call. "Christine Capper."

"Ah, Mr Fordice's big sister."

I frowned. Stephen Fordice was my younger brother, one of the better-known solicitors in Haxford. "Who is this?" I asked.

"Harold Aubrey, Mrs Capper… I'd like to hire your services as a private investigator. Are you free?"

"It depends how you interpret the word, Mr Aubrey, but the plain fact is a) I don't work free, and b) right now I have an appointment. I can be free in, say, an hour if that's convenient?"

"An hour will be fine, madam. Could you come to my office on Vulcan Street?"

"Two o'clock, then. I'll look forward to seeing you, Mr Aubrey."

Wondering what he wanted, persuading myself that it would be to do with the business at CutCost earlier in the day, I dropped the phone back in my pocket, and carried on to the Recorder offices. Less than a week to Christmas, and already things were becoming chaotic.

Chapter Four

Many, many moons ago, when we were both students at Haxford Technical College, I dated Ian Noiland, and as a consequence, I've often found him a useful source of information, but it wasn't as if I had any hold over him. Our teenage interaction never went anywhere further than heavy petting and roaming hands, or should I say, hands allowed to roam as far as I would permit, which wasn't very far.

After our brief conversation, I anticipated a meeting between the two of us, but I was mistaken. Lizzie Finister was sat alongside him when I walked in and took one of the visitor chairs opposite his desk.

Lizzie and I had a love-hate relationship. The previous Christmas, in direct contravention of local protocols, she named me when I was questioned on a murder. I retaliated by punching her in the mouth. Sometime just before Christmas last year, we called a truce, and earlier this year, I successfully pinned down the people who had drugged and murdered her father. That didn't make us bosom buddies, but it did smooth things over, and since then we'd enjoyed a more amicable relationship.

Having said that, she was still a reporter, and it was her job to cover the news, and as the Haxford Recorder's main crime correspondent, she didn't always let the truth inconvenience her articles.

I wasn't Ian's only visitor. Sat at the end of Ian's desk, to my right as I looked on, was a small, slender man somewhere in his mid-forties. Wearing little in the way of adornment other than a wristwatch, he had short, close trimmed, brown hair, a thin, well-tended beard with striking green eyes. I mean he had striking green eyes, not his beard.

Ian beamed a smile of welcome on me. "Afternoon, Chrissy. Allow me to introduce Norman Rushcroft."

Green eyes and beard also smiled. "A pleasure to meet you, Mrs Capper." He didn't offer to shake hands so I didn't either. I merely acknowledged him with a polite nod.

There was a brief hiatus while Ian's secretary supplied coffee, not as good as I made at home, but an improvement on some of the sludge you could buy in Haxford.

Once we were settled, Ian opened proceedings. "So, Chrissy, you're receiving messages from someone. Is it a murderer?"

Now I understood Lizzie's presence. He was hoping I might have a story for her.

"I didn't come here to listen to weak jokes, Ian," I said. "You know why I'm here."

He waved an open hand at Rushcroft. "Would you like to let Norman take a look at this message?"

My eye wandered to Rushcroft, I said, "I'm sorry, Ian, but I prefer not to discuss this matter in front of strangers."

"Norman isn't a stranger," Ian assured me.

I kept my eye on Rushcroft, and spoke to him directly. "So what are you, Mr Rushcroft? A technological whizzkid?"

"No, madam. I'm a former reporter turned freelance writer, and I'm a crossword compiler."

A broad smile crossed Ian's features. "I told you on the phone, Chrissy, Norman sets our crosswords, and I did say I'd ask him along."

Where was my brain? That was a question I asked myself. Of course Ian told me that Rushcroft was a freelance compiler.

"My apologies," I said, and opened up the text message before passing it to the puzzle prodigy.

He had a notepad alongside him, and began work on the text immediately.

While we waited, Ian asked, "No word on Harold Aubrey?"

"Funny you should mention him," I replied. "He rang me as I was making my way here. I'm meeting him at two o'clock."

I saw the fire come to Lizzie's eyes, but it was Ian who spoke first. "You're seeking legal advice? On crackpot text messages?"

"No. He needs my services as a private investigator."

That did it for Lizzie. "There's a story here, Ian," she said, and swung her excited eyes on me. "Any chance I can shadow you, Chrissy?"

"Two chances, Lizzie. Slim, and so remote that I'll win the lottery before it happens." I could feel my annoyance rising again. "After the Brophy business and your father's death at the beginning of the year, you should know by now, Lizzie, that all communication between me and my clients is privileged. I don't want a repeat of last Christmas when you told the world I'd been quizzed by the police."

She clucked. "How much longer do I have to pay for that mistake?"

"Consider it a penance," I advised, and then glanced at Rushcroft. His brow was creased and as I watched, he scrubbed through an entire line of text, and began writing afresh. "Everything all right, Mr Rushcroft?"

"Struggling a little, Mr Capper." He turned my phone towards me and used his pen as a pointer. "Hello catch nipper sire, is easy. It's simply, 'Hello Christine Capper'. Viz failed Dan wasn't clear until I realised today's date. It translates as *Feliz Navidad*, the Spanish for—"

"Merry Christmas," I cut him off. "Why wish me Merry Christmas in Spanish? It's not as if I know anyone in…"

My heart leapt as I trailed off. Ingrid and Darren. They were in Spain. Oh, my God, if someone had got to them…

To the astonishment and protests from the other three, I snatched my phone back, swept a finger over the lock screen, and hit the icon for Ingrid.

"Christine—"

I silenced Ian with an upraised finger as the phone began to ring out. It took an age before a groggy, sleepy Ingrid finally answered. "Mam, what the hell do you want? We didn't finish work until gone two this morning and we're back on stage at seven. We're trying to catch up on some sleep."

Relief flooded through me. "I'm sorry, love, but I've had a strange text today, and it's only just been analysed. Some barmpot was wishing me a Merry

Christmas in Spanish, and I was worried it might be hinting at someone having a go at you. I just needed to know you were safe."

"Aside from mothers disturbing our afternoon nap, we're fine. Now is that it?"

"For now. You just take care of yourselves. Keep an eye out for strangers stalking you."

"That's par for the course in Benidorm."

"All I'm saying is, be careful. Ring me later, just to let me know you're all right." I killed the call, and focused on Ian, Lizzie and Rushcroft. "I'm sorry about that. It was the Spanish phrase. It panicked me."

"Ingrid's in Spain?" Ian asked, and I was sure it was with an eye on a potential article.

"They've secured a full season in Benidorm."

"Could be an interesting local feature," he muttered. "Would she be prepared for an interview over Zoom?"

"You'd have to ask her," I replied. "Probably. They like the publicity, but she and Darren won't be back in this country until March next year, when the Scarborough caravan park opens again for the summer season." Determined to keep our focus, I handed the phone back to Rushcroft. "You said you were struggling?"

He screwed up his face, lips scrunched in, brow furrowed, lending him an almost simian appearance. "Hmm, yes. It's this phrase, 'for catch pet pay'. I'm not sure whether it's cryptic or clear English. If the latter, it means someone is asking you to pay for them to catch your pet. Tell me, madam, are you missing a pet?"

The worry came back to me. "As it happens, Cappy the Cat has gone missing this morning."

Rushcroft appeared taken aback. "Cappy? Curious name for a cat."

I tutted. "My husband, Dennis Capper, has a nickname. Cappy. When we got the cat, we decided to christen him Cappy, too. Problem was, Dennis never knew whether I was calling him or the cat, so we changed his name to Cappy the Cat. Changed the cat's name, that is. Not Dennis's. That way, when I call him for a feed, my husband doesn't turn up to feast on a tin of Whiskas."

With a bewildered shake of the head, Rushcroft returned to his puzzling, and a moment or two later, before I could get into any kind of exchange with Ian and Lizzie, he said, "Yes, I can see it now." He slid the phone back to me. "There are two ways of looking at this, Mrs Capper. First, it could be someone offering to catch and secure your cat, for a fee. Alternatively, the phrase, 'catch pet pay' could be translated as Cappy the Cat. In that instance, it sounds like someone is asking you to pay for the return of your pet."

My heart sank. It was exactly what Naomi said. "Are you suggesting someone has kidnapped my cat and is demanding a ransom?"

"That is one possibility. The complete text is vague. Were this a crossword, and you had other solutions in, you might be able to take a clue from individual letters, but of course, we have no such clues."

My thoughts settled on our local cattery. "Thank you, Mr Rushcroft. I've an idea where he might be.

I'll call on Bertha Ginsburgh after I've seen Harold Aubrey."

Lizzie laughed aloud. "Bertha? Putting together a text like that? Not this side of a millennium plus one. She's a plank."

"If you have any other ideas, Lizzie, I'm listening, and before you suggest Archie Prenton, I've already spoken to him. He hates Cappy the Cat and the feeling's mutual. But, antipathy aside, no one has left my missing moggie with him. Bertha's the only other option."

Determined not to be left out of the discussion, Ian chimed in, "I don't want to look on the dark side, Chrissy, but you do know that the law changed this year and pet abduction is a criminal offence."

I nodded. "Punishable by up to five years in prison," I said. Both Lizzie and Rushcroft appeared surprised and I felt obliged to explain myself to the crossword compiler. "Prior to this year, kidnapping pets was dealt with under the theft act, but the law changed to recognise the emotional impact of the crime, and as a cat lover, I'm wholly in favour of it." I got to my feet. "Thanks, Ian, Lizzie, Mr Rushcroft. I'd better get moving, see what Harold Aubrey has to say for himself."

Lizzie, too, stood up. "Wait on. I'll come with you."

"No, you won't, Lizzie."

"Yeah, but I can wait outside his office."

"Don't you understand the word confidential? I said no and I meant it."

She flopped back down again. "Well, don't forget to keep us up-to-date with whatever you learn. Cappy the Cat and Aubrey."

"Cappy the Cat, yes." I gave her a sickly smile. "Aubrey? Carry on dreaming." With that, I left them.

* * *

It's amazing how the cold hits you when you've been sat indoors for some time, isn't it? I stepped out into the street, and immediately began to shiver. Wrapping my coat round myself, pulling my woolly bonnet into place to keep my ears warm and prevent my dangly earrings from freezing to my neck, I turned back towards the town centre.

Aubrey's office was on Vulcan Street, a narrow thoroughfare, about 100 yards from the Recorder offices, and even if the car was anywhere nearby, it wouldn't be worth driving.

It was one of those narrow, tucked away, town centre streets. You know the kind I mean. Barely wide enough to accommodate a horse and cart, tall, redbrick buildings on either side, each housing professionals. Architects, accountants, a dentist, a podiatrist, and a small, cellar bar, branded, appropriately enough, The Cellar Bar. Not that I'd ever been a patron. As well as all these places, there were two solicitor's offices. Aubrey's at number seventeen, and my brother's place, at number thirty-six.

I was tempted to ring Stephen, ask about Aubrey before meeting the man, but I decided against it. In the early days of any consultation, it was as well to enter into it unbiased. If necessary, I could always speak to Stephen later.

For all that the street was mainly business rather than commercial, it was still busy, and as I made for Aubrey's place, shuffling through the crowds, I saw him and almost dropped on the spot.

As far as I knew, Nathan Kalinsky was serving life for murder. I helped send him down, and yet there he was, stood in the doorway of a secretarial agency, and he was looking straight at me. It was him. There was no mistaking the stocky, six-foot frame, the square-jawed, handsome features and the piercing blue eyes. He was the only man (aside from Dennis, obviously) who had got anywhere near my underwear in the last thirty years. And before you start demanding to know how that happened, it didn't. I stopped him. I'm not that kind of girl.

His twin brother, Sam, worked for some super-secret government department, and I knew he would have no business here in Haxford, so it had to be Nate.

It was disturbing. A man with a potential grudge against me, and a missing cat? Surely he wouldn't do that to get his revenge. Would he?

There was only one way to find out, and never let it be said that Christine Capper was a coward. Determined to confront him, I pushed and shoved my way through a small crowd of nuisances making for The Cellar Bar, and... he was gone.

Had I imagined it? Had that bizarre text message addled my brain?

Bewildered, more than a little disturbed, I turned back, and a few yards further on, I walked into Aubrey's outer office to be greeted by a young, smiling, blonde-haired woman who looked up from her typing. Judging from her age – late twenties in my opinion – I promptly wondered about the whisper I'd heard on the CutCost car park that morning. What did I say about remaining unbiased?

"Can I help you?" she asked.

"Christine Capper," I announced. "I have an appointment with Mr Aubrey for two o'clock."

She picked up her phone, muttered into it, then left her seat to guide me into the inner office.

As memory served, Harold Aubrey was in his late 40s, but a couple of years younger than my brother, who was 49 years of age. Notwithstanding that, Stephen was in much better condition than Mr Aubrey. This man was a shade taller than my 5'4", rotund, by which I mean fat, and his shabby, bagging suit was hardly befitting of a man charged with making representations to magistrates on behalf of his clients, and it appeared to me as if his shirt collar was trying to strangle him. It looked far too tight, or perhaps that was just my bias based on the ruddy colour of his chubby cheeks.

We shook hands, and he waved me to a seat opposite. "Would you like a cup of tea or something, Mrs Capper?"

"Kind of you, Mr Aubrey, but I'll pass if you don't mind. Too much tea in this weather sends me running to the little girls' room too often."

The weak joke was designed as an icebreaker, and it worked. Aubrey gave out a series of fat chuckles as he resumed his seat, and picked up the phone. "Jennifer," he said to his receptionist, "I don't want to be disturbed while I'm with Mrs

Capper."

I barely heard the receptionist/typist accede to the instruction.

Conscious of the time getting on and I still had to find Cappy the Cat, I pressed him. "So, Mr Aubrey, how can I help you?"

To be fair, he had no hesitation in speaking out. "Accusations have been laid against me, madam. Scurrilous accusations, designed, I believe to malign my reputation as both a legal practitioner and a gentlemen. They are nothing more than malicious allegations, totally untrue."

"And obviously, you've told the police this?"

"I have. They took me in for questioning this morning and they're looking into the matter, but at this moment in time, I remain released under interrogation, which as far as I'm concerned is only one step short of a criminal charge."

All well and good, but what was I supposed to do about it? Rather than running the question through my head, I put it to him. "What do you expect of me?"

"I'd like you to investigate, uncover the person who has made these allegations. The name has been mentioned to me, but frankly, I've never heard of this woman."

That final word alerted me. "The nature of the allegations, Mr Aubrey?"

He harrumphed. "I'd rather not go into details."

"In that case, there's nothing I can do. I'm sorry. I won't waste any more of your time." I was getting to my feet when he stayed me.

"All right, all right. Please. Sit down, please."

I resumed my seat. "Allow me to make my position clear? You know my brother, but I'm not sure how much Stephen might have told you about me. Many years ago, I was a police officer. I gave it up when I started a family. Then some years back, I took the professional investigation course which leaves me as Haxford's only licensed private investigator. I'm governed by a non-statutory body, but one which has the power to strike me from their register if I step out of line. Part and parcel of their regime is absolute client confidentiality. I am duty-bound to maintain any information you give me in the strictest secrecy. I can only reveal that information to the police, and only then on production of a court order. There are exemptions to that rule, Mr Aubrey, the main one being criminal activity. If I suspect such activity in any client, then it's my civic duty to report the matter to the police. Let's take this a little further. I don't know what's been said about you, I don't know what you've been accused of, but if these allegations are untrue, then I'm likely to be treading on police toes. That's not a problem as far as I'm concerned, but I need to be aware of the danger of transgressing the law myself. I have to know about these allegations, where they came from, who made them. Without that background, I can't help. Are we clear on this?"

He was resigned to it. "I fully appreciate your position, madam." Even in capitulation it took him a good half minute before he went into his explanation. "A woman named Trea Chapel has alleged that I have been harassing her. It isn't true, Mrs Capper. I don't know anyone by that name. She certainly isn't a client of mine. I've never heard of her, and when the police showed me the messages they received from this woman, I didn't recognise the telephone number. I made this point to Detective Sergeant Hiscoe, and to Detective Constable Capper, who I believe is your son. They have to investigate. That goes without saying, but privately both Ms Hiscoe and your young man advised me to contact you."

I nodded my understanding, if only to demonstrate that I'd be listening. "Mandy and I are old friends, but that doesn't mean she'll be happy to show me these messages. Did she allow you to copy them out?"

"She did not."

"This woman claims that you've been harassing her. Does that mean sexual harassment?"

"Yes. It does. I didn't mention it because I didn't want to embarrass you."

I almost laughed. "You'll find it very difficult to embarrass me," I lied. In fact, with my attitude towards naughty business, I was the easiest person in the world to embarrass, and as I sat there, the Allbrook business came back to me. Some of those messages were the most disgusting I'd ever read.

"Forgive me if I sound a little too sceptical, but has this ever happened to you before?"

I thought he would explode. Given the size of his waistline, it wouldn't surprise me if he did, and I was ready to duck from a welter of blood and guts coming my way. His features turned even redder, and his dander came up. "Of course not. I'm a respectable, married man, a professional lawyer. I have never, in all my years as a practising solicitor, made any improper advances to anyone. And if you don't believe me, try asking my wife. No one knows me better than Faith. This... this Trea Chapel is making mischief, and I don't understand why. For God's sake, as I've already said, I don't even know her."

"Curious name, too, isn't it? Trea." It was an aside, designed to help him calm down.

"Irish, as I understand it. It roughly translates as strength."

I came to a decision there and then. "All right, Mr Aubrey, I'll take your case. May I detail my charges?"

He nodded, I went into the fees – £50 per hour plus any out-of-pocket expenses – and I concluded by saying, "I'll get onto Mandy Hiscoe, see what I can learn from her, but if they won't let me see these messages, I'm going to have to ask you to secure them. As you say, you're a lawyer, you must know ways and means of getting around these restrictions." I dug into my bag, brought out a business card and handed it to him. "If you can get them, the moment you have them, email or text them to me, and I'll take it from there."

We shook hands on the deal, and satisfied that I had a nice little earner, as Dennis like to describe such work, to help with the Christmas bills, I came back out into the cold.

Next stop, Bertha Ginsburgh's cattery and what I fancied would be another chilly, head-to-head.

Chapter Five

Driving out of Haxford towards Huddersfield, it's mostly built up, residential and commercial areas, but there's a stretch about a mile and a half out of Haxford where you come into sort of wooded countryside where the moors are invisible behind the wall of trees either side of the road. Another mile or two further on and you're coming back into civilization on the southern outskirts of Huddersfield, but Ginsburgh's Cattery was located in that short, rural gap.

It wasn't a large place. Just an old, stone-built house with a large (heated) outbuilding attached to it where the cats were boarded. She kept a few chickens but I'd always suspected she also slaughtered and plucked them. I always felt that it was cheaper, cleaner and less yukky to buy frozen chicken at CutCost, but then, I imagine Bertha needed some outlet for her inherent ferocity. And that aspect of her personality wasn't exclusively down to my overactive imagination. Some time back, there was a report of a break-in at her place. The police had to wait 24 hours in A&E before they could interview the burglar after Bertha caught and restrained him. I say restrained when what I mean was battered him. She wasn't prosecuted for it either. I suppose they couldn't find a magistrate with the courage to face her across the courts.

At about £15 per night, putting our moody moggie into a cattery cost more than the price of a week's stay in an off-season caravan on Turpin's

Park where Ingrid and Darren spent their summers, so we tended to make do with Simon and Naomi, and latterly, Hazel McQuarrie. On occasion, however, when they were not available, we had used Bertha Ginsburgh's services, and it didn't take her long to decide that she didn't like Cappy the Cat.

Wearing a humongous bib and brace overall, she emerged from the house as I pulled into her small parking area, and when I climbed out of the car, she greeted me, "I'm only taking strays in over Christmas."

This was a curious counterpoint to her general personality. It was no secret that she did not like people, but she adored cats, and although she charged for her boarding services, she was always ready to take in stray felines.

When she made her announcement, I felt relieved that I wasn't a stray.

"Good afternoon, Bertha," I said, determined to remain as pleasant as possible. "I'm not looking to board my cat. In fact, I'm wondering whether anyone's dropped him off, thinking he might be a stray."

"I didn't know there were that many suicidal people in Haxford. Anyone trying to pick up that vicious velocipede of yours would have had their hands stripped to the bone."

For 'velocipede' I read velociraptor. "So you haven't seen him then?"

"Didn't I just say so?"

I could feel my irritation rising. "No, you didn't. You just denounced him as a nasty piece of work."

"He is a nasty piece of work."

"He's a match for you then, isn't he?" I dug out a business card and handed it to her. "If anyone should bring him in, would you be kind enough to ring me?"

"If I can find the time." At that, she turned back into the house.

Feeling even more annoyed, I climbed back into my car, and as I got behind the wheel, making an effort to dismiss Bertha's bad mood and manners, I made an effort to focus on Harold Aubrey's problem. I needed to speak to Mandy (she was always freer with information than my son) and my brother. Mandy would be forthcoming on the allegations made against Aubrey, and Stephen would know more about the man.

I took out my phone, and as I prepared to make the first call to Mandy, the thing tweeted to indicate an incoming text message.

I don't mind admitting that I opened it with some trepidation, fully justified a couple of seconds later when I read the message.

With every missive it goes up, crit paper inches. Feel I fuel onions is now a grand in my hand. Loan tea bun.

My pulse rate went through the roof, and I had to carry out a series of deep breathing exercises to help me calm down.

A moment or two later, with some semblance of rational thought taking over, I looked again at the message, and at least one of the idiotic phrases was easy to translate. 'Crit paper inches' was Christine Capper. 'A grand in my hand' definitely sounded like a ransom demand, which indicated that Cappy the Cat had indeed been kidnapped. 'Feel I fuel onions' and 'loan tea bun' were total mysteries to me. They were a job for Norman Rushcroft.

I glanced over my shoulder, back at Bertha's place, and I could see her stood in the window, watching me. Was it possible? Here I was, looking for my precious pet, the moment I mentioned it to her, she denied having seen anything of him, and then suddenly I received another text message.

Lizzie had insisted that Bertha didn't have the level of intelligence needed to construct this kind of complicated message, but my many years of experience both as a police officer and a private investigator had told me just how deceptive appearance could be. She was a good few years older than me, and I didn't remember her from my childhood (why would I when she lived so far out of town?) and I didn't recall ever seeing her at school. It was entirely possible that she had an intellect as gargantuan as her body, and judging from the comparative squalor in which she lived, she wouldn't be shy of demanding money with menaces.

I stopped the engine, climbed out of the car again, marched up to the door, and rattled the knocker. She opened it so quickly that I thought she was trying to tear it off its hinges.

"What do you want?"

Time, I decided, that she learned she didn't have a monopoly on anger. "Have you just sent me a stupid text message?"

"Why would I?"

"You tell me. I'm looking for my cat, and I think you've got him hidden in the shed of yours."

She pushed past me, marched to the shed, threw open the door, and then challenged me. "Take a look, you silly cow. Your terrorist tomcat isn't here."

Ever the more determined not to back down, I did as she demanded.

The place was decked out with cages, stacked up almost to the ceiling, and lining all the walls. There were no more than half a dozen cats in residence, and I assumed that they were the strays she mentioned earlier. Whatever their pedigree, Cappy the Cat was not amongst them.

I turned on my heel and marched out to face up to her. "Someone has my cat, and if I find out it's you, you'll learn what it is to take on someone who's more than you can handle."

I returned to my car, started the engine, yanked my seatbelt into place, and drove out onto the road, heading back to Haxford.

Dennis and I had been together for three decades, and in reality, I couldn't wish for a better husband, but there were those times when he annoyed me, and as I drove along, this was one of them. I needed to speak to Mandy Hiscoe, but Dennis had never got round to fixing up my car with a mobile hands-free set up. It meant pulling into a little parking spot half a mile along the road, and ringing Mandy from there.

"Whatever you want, Chrissy, the answer's no."

"How do you know? I might have won the lottery and be offering you a half share."

"It's five days to Christmas, and we're running round in ever decreasing circles. What do you want?"

"Half an hour of your time. I'm receiving text messages—"

"I know. You told me at CutCost this morning."

"They're threatening, Mandy. I'm sure of it. Please, spare me even a few minutes."

She sighed. "I'm at the station. Come on down."

"Give me twenty minutes." I cut the call, and rang Ian at the Recorder. "It's your favourite private eye. I've received another message. Is your super-duper puzzler still with you?"

"No. He's gone home. What's wrong? Received another message did you say?"

"Yes. I think I've got some of it, but there's a couple of things I can't work out."

"Tell you what, Chrissy. Send it to me and I'll forward it to Norman. With a bit of luck, I'll have an answer for you later this afternoon. Any news on Harold Aubrey?"

"No. Come on, Ian. You're getting as bad as Lizzie. When I can tell you something, I'll tell you, but not until. I'll forward the message to you."

Once I'd forwarded the message, I set up again, and fifteen minutes later, I climbed out of the car and walked into Haxford police station where I was greeted by a surly Vic Hillman.

"We don't have time for you today, Capper. Clear off."

"I'm here to see Mandy, and she's expecting me. So knock it off, Minx, and let her know I'm here."

He picked up the phone and as he dialled, he

warned, "Don't call me Minx."

"You know, Minx, I'm glad your name is Hillman and not Ford. As nicknames go, Fiesta wouldn't suit you."

A few minutes later, I sat with Mandy in her little office, and she looked over the two text messages.

"They're garbage," she announced.

"Not so," I disagreed. "I've had the first one analysed, and there's a couple of possible solutions. The second one seems to be reinforcing the general opinion of the first. Someone, Mandy, has bagged my cat and then demanding an increasing ransom. The first one, if you read it, says 'let's say an even five', the second one reinforces that with the phrase, 'a grand in my hand'."

She tutted. "Seriously, Chrissy, do you know how busy we are?"

"Of course I do, but if I'm right, if the analyses are right, then this is pet abduction, and I shouldn't need to remind you, Mandy, that that is a crime."

"True, but you can't confirm it yet." She waved an open hand at the smartphone now laid on her desk. "Like I said, this is nonsense. If it was plain English, if someone was seriously demanding a thousand pounds for the return of your pet, then fine. But the best I can offer right now is to make a note of it until we're definite. Then I can record it as a crime. Mind you, even then, I don't know that we'll find the time or the personnel to look into it."

She was right. I knew she was right. Even in those far-off days when I walked the beat in Haxford, the police were always under intense pressure.

"Very well. I'll look into it myself, but I'm telling you, Mandy, once I know for certain, I'll expect you to take whatever action is possible, even if that's only reporting it." I picked up my phone and took a couple of deep breaths to calm down for the umpteenth time during that day. "While I'm here, Harold Aubrey has hired me to track down this person accusing him of harassment. What can you tell me?"

"Technically? Legally? Nothing. Between you, me, and these four walls, it does look like a malicious allegation. I don't believe there's any semblance of truth in it, and we can't find a single trace of this Trea Chapel."

"Any danger I could see the allegation?"

"Nothing to see. The woman phoned it in, and gave us precise details of what had – allegedly – happened. While Simon and I pulled Aubrey in this morning, I sent Fliss Keele out to the woman's address, and guess what... No such person."

"Interesting." I marshalled my thoughts. "What do you know about Harold Aubrey? I mean, is he that way inclined?"

The hangdog expression returned to her face. "Whisper is that he used to be. I think he's getting too old now, but he did have a bit of a rep for playing the field. Know what I mean? Have you ever met his wife?"

"No."

"Faith. Shocking snob, and between you and me, I think she makes his life hell. Well, she did do when they were younger. That might account for his waywardness back in the day. Nowadays, frankly, he's too old, too fat, too unattractive to even try it."

I tutted. "He's younger than my brother."

"Yes, I know, but if I was scouting for a sugar-daddy, your brother would be a better proposition."

We left it at that. Stephen's wife, Melinda, my airs and graces sister-in-law, wasn't maybe so bad as Faith Aubrey sounded, but she still made what I considered unreasonable demands on my brother, demands like keeping expensive champagne in the house at all times. Not exactly Dom Perignon, but a few rungs up the ladder from supermarket bubbly.

As I came out of the police station, it occurred to me that Faith Aubrey might give me some clue to the woman accusing her husband. A quick call to my friend Kim Aspinall at the library confirmed that the Aubreys lived in a large, detached house on the west side of Haxford, not far from The Cottage, our local name for the Haxford Cottage Hospital. It was the affluent quarter, and when I got there, that was reflected in the neatly trimmed lawns and flowerbeds, looking sad and sorry in their post-winter poverty, but nevertheless clearly marked out.

I found a white Peugeot people carrier parked in the drive, its bodywork gleaming even in the dull light of a December afternoon. Inside, the place was awash with Christmas decorations (well, it would be, wouldn't it?) and the lights of a fake tree twinkled through the early afternoon gloom.

According to my estimate, Faith Aubrey was in her late forties, much like her husband. A bottle blonde whose dark roots showed where her hair was parted at the crown. She sat before a mock fireplace in the grandly furnished and decorated front room, her fingers entangled in a handkerchief. Somewhere during the day, she had applied make-up, but it was running, streaked with tears, and when I sat with her, the blue eyes sparkled as if she were ready to cry once more.

She was sceptical about letting me in but eventually agreed and when I finally sat opposite her, explained that I was a private investigator and that her husband had hired me, her anger burst through. "The police asked, and I told them it'll be that bitch, Jennifer bloody Vetch."

The moment I heard the name, I almost jumped out of my skin. Vetch. A rare and unusual name, and by coincidence, the surname of one of Dennis's partners. Or was it a coincidence?

I controlled the impulse to get up and leave. Forcing calm upon myself, I asked, "Jennifer Vetch? What is she to your husband? And I'm sorry, I don't mean is she a lover or anything. I mean does he know her as part of his routine working life or something? Was she ever a colleague or a client?"

"She's his secretary and receptionist."

"Oh."

I had to focus my attention again. "And are you aware of any liaison between them?"

"Liaison?" Faith laughed harshly. "Is that the politically correct name for (bleep)?"

I censored the final word. It brought a rush of colour to my ears and cheeks.

Faith's lapse into street vernacular was enunciated with the high and precise, Queen's

English with which she had greeted me. Anger, I diagnosed. It had a way of betraying ones roots. It was my guess that Faith Aubrey came from a working class, or at best, lower middle-class background, and her linguistic affectations were a much later adornment, designed to ensure her husband's better off clients accepted her as one of their caste.

She was not done. "She's been after him for at least a year, perhaps longer. I'm not stupid, Mrs Capper. I know all about women like her."

"And you never queried it with your husband?"

"I have Octavia and Quincy, my son and daughter, to think about."

As if to lend weight to my previous assessment, the children's names suggested an extreme of self-importance. Faith Aubrey was a cut above the rest, and intended that everyone should know it even if that meant lumbering her children with pretentious names.

I could probably forgive her for that, but not for her failure to tackle him on his affair – assuming the affair existed in reality rather than her mind.

I focussed my attention. "If I may ask, why would this Jennifer Vetch harass your husband in this manner?"

"Because he wouldn't sleep with her, obviously."

It was anything but obvious to me.

Faith was still pressing her point. "He may be getting on, but he's still quite a catch, you know."

Yes, I thought, in the same way that Moby Dick was quite a catch for Captain Ahab. I got the impression that Faith Aubrey was looking at her husband through glasses tinted with a large £ sign. Maybe she wasn't so different to my brother's wife.

"You can't think anyone else who might have had a grudge against your husband. A grudge strong enough to smear his reputation?"

"No. It was the Vetch tart. I guarantee it."

It was obvious to me that I wouldn't learn anything more from her. I took a business card from my bag and passed it to her. "Obviously, Mrs Aubrey, I'm not the police. They are investigating, but your husband is paying me to make inquiries too, so if you can think of anything else that you might be able to tell me, or if you need any assistance at all, please, don't hesitate to call me."

She took the card and tossed it to one side on an occasional table. "I think I can safely leave it to the police. They know who the woman is, they know what she's about and I'm sure they'll have her under lock and key before the day's out."

I wouldn't bet on it. That was the thought ringing round my head, as I left her and got back into my car.

Chapter Six

It was past four o'clock and darkness had already fallen when I climbed back into my car, my mind a tumult, thoughts cascading from all directions, effectively blocking out the capacity for logical, reasonable planning.

I had two problems. Not counting Christmas preparations, that is. First, Cappy the Cat. Where was he, who had him, were the text messages really a demand for ransom, or simple nuisance? Second, Harold Aubrey. Who was Trea Chapel? And how, if at all, did Jennifer Vetch figure in Aubrey's problems? Were her supposed designs upon Faith's husband no more than the wife's fantasy, or was there some truth in them?

I knew who she was. Well, I say I knew. What I mean is, I was practically certain. Vetch wasn't the most common name in Haxford, or even Great Britain, and I knew of only one family. Greg Vetch, one of Dennis's partners at Haxford Fixers, his ex-wife, and any children he might have.

Of Dennis's three business partners, I knew Tony Wharrier and Lester Grimes really well. My acquaintance with them went back to the days when they first set up Haxford Fixers. I didn't know Greg, who was brought in after Dennis was badly beaten up during the by-election fiasco, quite so well. What I did know was that he was pleasant, easy to get on with, supportive, and like all the Haxford Fixers' partners, hard-working. Correction, three of the partners were hard-working; Dennis, Tony, and

Greg. Lester did only as much as he needed to in order to earn enough money for his tobacco and his nightly beer at the Engine House pub.

Even at this hour, I knew they would be hard at work and I could catch them at their workshop if I wanted, but said workshop was in Haxford Mill, the other side of town, and I really didn't fancy battling with the increasing rush-hour traffic to get there. I had to fight with the traffic anyway, in order to get home, which was broadly speaking in the same direction, but having to go that extra mile purely to speak to Greg, and then double back to go home did not appeal.

I was still dithering over it when the phone rang. Ian at the Recorder. I made the connection. "What can I do for you, Ian?"

"Are you busy, Chrissy?"

"Twiddling my thumbs, trying to decide whether to go to Haxford Mill to see my old man and his partners, or to go home."

"It might be better if you make your way to our office. We've got news for you, and it doesn't sound too good."

Honestly, if I had any more anxiety attacks that day, I swear they would bring on a heart attack. "The latest text?"

"What else? Norman's with me. He's got an answer for you and I don't think you're going to like it." He sucked in a breath, a sure sign that the news was the worst. "It sounds like someone has kidnapped your cat."

"I'll be with you in a quarter of an hour...traffic permitting."

With typical Haxford obduracy, it took me almost twenty minutes to get to the market car park, and then another five or ten minutes walking through the icy cold streets, threading my way through crowds of people, many of them trying to get home from work, a good proportion still hurrying round to get their last minute purchases before the shops closed for the night.

All up then, I was grateful for a mug of inadequate coffee when I joined Ian, Lizzie, and Norman Rushcroft.

I dispensed with polite preliminaries and focused on the crossword king. "Ian says you have an answer for me, Mr Rushcroft?"

"Indeed, madam. Allow me to reiterate the message." He looked down at his notes. "With every missive it goes up, crit paper inches. Feel I fuel onions is now a grand in my hand. Loan tea bun." He fixed my eye. "The opening is fairly simple. It reads, with every message, the price goes up, and it addresses you by name. Crit paper inches readily translates as Christine Capper. Because the first message contained the Spanish greeting, *Feliz Navidad*, 'loan tea bun' was simple enough to translate as *Buon Natale*, Merry Christmas in Italian. The only thing I struggled with was, 'feel I fuel onions'. Needless to say, I cracked it." He checked his notes again. "It reads, 'felonious feline'. Replacing that, Mrs Capper, the full message translates as, 'with every message, the price goes up, Christine Capper. Felonious feline is now a grand in my hand. Merry Christmas'." Rushcroft looked up yet again and focused on me.

"I take that to mean that the first message was demanding five hundred pounds, and now he – or she – is demanding one thousand pounds. Your cat, Mrs Capper, has been abducted."

I was a flood of different emotions. Murderous fury, countered by debilitating anxiety, the desire to go out and buy a gun and shoot this evil person, the need to see, stroke, cuddle my pet again. Not that Cappy the Cat would ever allow me to cuddle him, but you know what I mean.

Ian, Lizzie, Rushcroft, all remained silent, waiting for me to come back to them, but I had nothing to say. At length, Ian broke the silence.

"Did you check on Bertha Ginsburgh?" After I gave him a nod by return, he asked, "Did you report it to Mandy Hiscoe?"

I cleared my throat. "I did. She can't take any action."

"Why the hell not?" Lizzie demanded. "You said earlier that pet abduction is an offence in its own right these days."

I gestured at Rushcroft. "It's the format of the messages. They're cryptic. Open to interpretation, and although I'm not doubting Mr Rushcroft's efforts, it's entirely possible that there are other interpretations. That being the case, until she has some definitive… I hesitate to use the word proof, but certainly I mean strong evidence. Until she has that, she can't do anything. It's down to me."

Lizzie was immediately on the front foot. "Not likely. Listen, Chrissy, I know you shouted me down before, but I haven't forgot what you did for me earlier this year. I'm pleading with you to let me shadow you. I promise nothing will appear in print until I have your say so."

I remained hesitant. "I don't know, Lizzie."

"Well, it makes sense to me," Ian insisted. "Suppose you come up against this clown, and he's bigger, tougher than you?"

"As big as Bertha Ginsburgh," Lizzie suggested.

Ian pressed on. "You're gonna need some assistance. And, think on this. If you can crack it, this side of Christmas, it'll make a great story for the Recorder. Most of the town will end up in your corner."

I hesitated still, even though I'd already decided to drag Lizzie along. It wasn't her presence which caused my silence. It was something that had occurred to me while Ian was in full persuasion mode.

I turned to Rushcroft. "May I ask, how long it took you to crack that felonious feline anagram?"

He pursed his lips. "I suppose, ten minutes, perhaps a little less."

I mirrored his pursed lips. "Impressive. I don't think I could have done it in ten years."

There must have been something in my voice which hinted at my doubts. His brow creased, his eyes narrowed, and he asked, "Is there something on your mind, Mrs Capper?"

"Hmm, yes. What's occurred to me, Mr Rushcroft, is that cracking a seriously difficult clue like that in such a short time would be so much easier for someone who composed it in the first place." Before they could shout me down, I pressed my attack. "How do you feel about cats and their owners, Mr Rushcroft?"

Earlier in the day, I'd assessed him as small, weedy, a little backward in coming forward. But now he stood and raised himself to his full height (about 5'3" according to my calculations). "I resent that, madam," he hissed. "I am a respected writer, journalist and crossword compiler, not a common criminal, and I can't remember any time when I was so insulted as by your words."

It was on the tip of my tongue to say, 'well, you should get out more,' but I refrained, and he ranted on.

"Mr Noiland called me in to break down these messages, madam, because cryptic clues, anagrams, and the like are one of my specialities. I resent the imputation that I may be the one behind them. In order to help me break these messages down, I need information, which you, Mr Noiland and Ms Finister have supplied. From there, the messages are not too difficult to analyse. Let's take, for example, the line in this morning's first message, loan tea bun. There are several possible answers to that simple phrase, but as I've already explained, bearing in mind that the first message contained the Spanish greeting *Feliz Navidad*, it was quite simple to translate this as *Buon Natale*, the Italian for Merry Christmas."

I was taken aback by the ferocity in his response. I had him down as a sort of mild mannered gentlemen, one who reminded me of Clark Kent, except that Norman Rushcroft bore no resemblance to Superman. More like super-weedy nerd. That was assuming he did not put all the messages together in the first place, and I refused to accept that as definite.

In a show of determination, I responded, "I'll keep all my options open, thank you, Mr Rushcroft. For now, I'll offer my thanks for cracking the two final phrases I couldn't get to. But, there's something you should know about me, something Ian and Lizzie may have neglected to mention. I don't run away. I don't turn my back on any possibility, including the chance that you might be the one behind all this." I was sure he was about to respond, but I didn't give him the chance. Instead, I turned to Ian. "I don't think there's much more to be said or done here, Ian, so I'll shoot off to the Market Tavern for a quick drink and try to calm down. Fancy coming with me, Lizzie?"

"Give me a coupla minutes, Chrissy."

I agreed, picked up my phone, and left Ian's office to wait outside. I was going to chat with his secretary about up-and-coming Christmas, but I never got the chance. Rushcroft followed me out and confronted me.

"Do you understand the term slander, Mrs Capper?"

"I was a police officer so of course I do. But do you understand, Mr Rushcroft, that for any accusation to be slanderous, it has to be repeated in front of others, and the only two people I've repeated it to are those employing you, and even they argued. Once upon a time, I foolishly took on work for Gus Leach, the man who owned Jumping Jacks before he died. He asked me to gather evidence of his wife's infidelity. When I learned what kind of man he was, I tried to back out, but he wouldn't let me. Instead, he had one of his thugs threaten me. The point I'm trying to make, Mr Rushcroft is that I didn't run away when he set his goons on me."

"Old history. And that's nothing—"

An idea occurred to me. It came straight out of nowhere, but it made a kind of warped sense to me, and I cut Rushcroft off. "Have you ever employed Harold Aubrey?"

"I… er… I think he dealt with my late mother's estate."

"Did he let you down?" I didn't wait for an answer because I suspected it would be a flat, 'no'. And anyway, Lizzie came out of Ian's office right then. "Thank you for your time and effort, Mr Rushcroft. If I'm wrong about you, then I will, of course, apologise, but right now, as far as I'm concerned, you remain a person of interest. I'll bid you good day. Are you fit, Lizzie?"

"I'm not throwing a fit like you, but I'm ready. See you later, Norman."

Lizzie's glib tone wasn't lost on me, and nor was her friendly *adieu* to Rushcroft. I challenged her on it the moment we were out on the street. "You don't agree with me, do you?"

"What? About Norm? To be honest, Chrissy, I've never seen him that het up. You really rattled his cage. For a minute there, I expected him to burst into tears. And think about it. I can see him strangling a cat. It would be the right size of target for him if he was in a paddy, but I can't see him nicking one and demanding a ransom."

I knew she was wrong, but as we walked along, I didn't know what I could say to persuade her.

Battling through the early evening crowds, pausing now and then to take in spectacular, Christmas window displays, I happened to glance across at the entrance to Home Bargains, and that's when I saw her.

For the second time that day, I had to question my sanity. Like my (apparent) sighting of Nathan Kalinsky earlier in the afternoon, this could not be right. She, like Nate, was in prison, serving life. How could she be stood outside Home Bargains?

I looked away, look back again, and she was still there, and although it was difficult to tell in the darkness, I was sure she was looking straight at me. I was about to go across and challenge her, when I looked to the large newsagents on the opposite side of the street, and he was there, Nate. Again. But he wasn't looking at me this time. He was studying her.

A crowd of early drinkers pushed their way past us, and once they were gone, I took two steps in her direction, and... She was gone. Fair enough. I would challenge him instead, but when I looked, he, too had gone.

Was I losing my mind? Was my missing cat and the supposed threat to him causing hallucinations?

"What's up, Chrissy?" Lizzie asked.

"I, er, I don't know. I'm seeing things, Lizzie. Seeing people who aren't there."

She laughed. "Sounds to me like you need a drink. Come on."

This second apparition of the day preyed on my

mind, until we got to the Market Tavern, where I struggled through the crowds and secured us a tiny table in one corner while she went to the bar for drinks: a G&T for her, a non-alcoholic white wine spritzer for me. I'd have preferred Bacardi, but I had to drive home yet, and as for letting her pay, well, she had a more regular income than me. She was salaried, I was self-employed.

The place was heaving, most of the patrons just out of their day's work and on their theoretical way home but in need of a snifter to fortify them for the traffic battle. Many of the tables were cluttered with gaily decorated Christmas shopping bags, most of them bursting at the seams. It served to remind me that I still had a mass of shopping to do.

Even as I thought of it, the prospect was displaced by a vision of Cappy the Cat wearing a Santa hat. I still had a photograph of him like that on my phone. It wasn't real. When I tried to put a little Santa bonnet on him, one hiss and a single sweep of his paw was enough to remove it. In the end, I doctored the photograph online. Even so, it provided some entertainment for my social media followers, and if nothing else, thinking about it helped me forget about my ghosts of Christmas past.

Lizzie helped, too. Cappy the Cat was on her mind when she finally wriggled into her seat. Or rather, my allegations against Rushcroft were occupying her thoughts. "You don't seriously think it's Norm, do you?"

"As I said, I prefer to keep all options in mind," I replied as I sipped from my spritzer. "He got to those answers too quickly for my liking."

"Yes, but like I told you, that's his bag."

"I don't recall you saying anything of the kind."

"Didn't I? Well, I meant to." She gulped down a mouthful of gin and topped up the remainder from her bottle of tonic. "My full name, Elizabeth Finister, might be easy to turn into some kind of anagram, but my preferred name, Lizzie Finister, isn't. The best I could come up with was more of a spoonerism; Fizzy Linister. So I once bet Norm a bottle of scotch against a bottle of Bacardi that he couldn't come up with an anagram of my name. My shortened name, that is. It took him less than five minutes. I quote, I lit fez sizer in."

"And was it right?"

"Bang on. Ian refereed the bet, and it cost me a bottle of Johnnie Walker. It doesn't make much sense in English, but how many anagrams do. What was that in your latest message? Loan tea bun. It's nonsense, isn't it? But it still translated into Merry Christmas in Spanish."

"Italian," I corrected her. "The Spanish version was first thing."

"Whatever. All I'm saying, Chrissy, is the man is an absolute genius when it comes to this kind of rubbish. Words, playing about with them, are his thing. I know that doesn't make a lot of difference to you, because whoever's doing this has the same talent, but it's my broader knowledge of Norman Rushcroft that tells me he won't have nicked your cat." Another slug of gin and tonic disappeared. "Course, I can't say the same for Bertha Ginsburgh."

I shook my head. "Been there, done that, and Cappy the Cat isn't there."

Lizzie was not persuaded. "You mean she let you look in the shed where she keeps the cats she's boarding. She might look stupid, but I'll bet she isn't, and if she's hijacked your Cappy, she'll have kept him in the house. Bet she didn't let you look there, did she?"

I was forced to agree. "Why would she, though, Lizzie? I mean, she doesn't like Cappy the Cat. She admitted as much. But generally speaking she's a cat lover."

"She's also skint."

The announcement took me by surprise. "Never," I argued. "She has that house, the land around it, crikey, she must be worth a fortune."

"Yes, but it's all tied up in the house and the land. I'm not saying I've got this right, Chrissy, but she could be seriously strapped for cash. I mean, how many people need their cats boarding at this time of year? Correction. How many people in Haxford need their cats boarding at this time of year? There's not much money in this town so we don't get many of them floating off abroad for the Christmas holidays, do we?"

Again I had to agree. "No. Only people like my neighbour, Hazel McQuarrie."

Lizzie laughed. "The frisky old widow? Where's she going?"

"Tenerife. Tomorrow morning." I wasn't about to let the debate drift. "You're suggesting that Bertha Ginsburgh might have kidnapped Cappy the Cat? But does she have enough brains to put together complicated text messages like those I'm receiving? I did challenge her on it, but she denied it point-blank."

"Well, she would, wouldn't she? I just said, didn't I, don't know that I'm right, but it's more of a possibility than Norman Rushcroft."

I checked the time above the bar and wolfed down the remainder of my spritzer. "Whatever. It'll have to wait until tomorrow now. I'm on my way home, and I guarantee I'll walk into another argument."

"Dennis?" she asked.

I nodded. "He's always been a dog lover. He doesn't like Cappy the Cat."

That brought another chuckle from Lizzie. "You sure he hasn't bagged your moggie?"

"That makes even less sense than Bertha Ginsburgh. Dennis would never demand a ransom for the cat because he'd have to pay it." I got to my feet. "I'll catch you later, Lizzie. I'll ring first thing in the morning, and we'll make arrangements."

Chapter Seven

When I got back to the car I settled behind the wheel, switched on the engine, and I was about to drive off, when I changed my mind. I left the engine running, combating the icy night, and for many minutes, I sat staring through the windscreen, watching the people coming and going.

According to the dashboard clock it was coming up to six, and there was a noticeable change amongst the crowds milling around the market area. Many were still laden with their Christmas purchases, but others were already out, in their party pants, ready to make an early start to the evening's enjoyment. A typical Friday evening.

Friday? What was I thinking? It was only Thursday, and these party people were obviously determined to make an early start to Christmas.

The full impact hit me. This nightmare, which I felt I'd been suffering for the last forty-eight hours, was actually less than ten hours old, and during that short space of time I'd been zipping around Haxford, backwards, forwards, backwards, forwards, and driven halfway to Huddersfield and back.

The day's events flashed through my mind like a video replay on fast forward, individual scenes coming to the fore for the briefest of moments, and it served to underscore the core problem. Cappy the Cat.

I still had no definitive evidence, let alone proof that someone had taken my pet, but I was resigned to it. Why were people so cruel? All right, so dealing with Cappy the Cat tended to be less pleasant than helping Dennis cut his toenails, but he was my cat, my (distant) companion, a fixture in my life upon whom I… I wouldn't say doted, but he was there, and it was one of my roles, my duty to take care of him, feed him, groom him (when he would allow) and no one had the right to rob me of his presence nor to deprive him of my attention.

I pulled away from the car park, dropped onto Yorkshire Street, heading south, joining the homeward bound throng of traffic, and I swear I saw her again, standing outside the library this time. When the traffic ground to a halt, I looked again, and she wasn't there.

A feeling of desolation enveloped me. The ghosts of people who were locked away in prison, a missing cat, I prayed it was all nothing worse than stress.

Cappy the Cat was a kitten when we first picked him up, one of a sizeable litter, and his mother's owner had no clue which particular tomcat had impregnated her pet. She just wanted rid of the kittens as soon as they were old enough to leave the care of the she cat. He had no pedigree, but from day one he made it plain who was in charge. There's an old adage. When you own a dog, you are the owner, but when you own a cat, you are the servant and he/she owns you. That was certainly the case with Cappy the Cat. Even as he grew through feline adolescence, he ruled the roost, not only indoors, but in the general area of Bracken Close. Dogs, even large mutts soon learned to give him a wide berth. We had no trouble with mice, certainly none with rats, and other rodents such as squirrels were quick to jump up into the trees and clear off when Cappy the Cat was on patrol. The only creatures which beat him were the birds, the sparrows, starlings, pigeons, magpies who visited the suspended feeder in our back garden. Even then, our tyrant tomcat made strenuous efforts to jump up and catch them.

And he didn't behave like other cats. There are those people on social media who say their cats follow them everywhere. Cappy the Cat didn't. I recall one woman complaining that her cat often followed her into the shower. Mine never did. Aside from drinking it, he hated water with the same passion that he hated almost everything and everyone else, and at those times when I had to bath him, he struggled, wriggled, brought out his lethally sharpened claws, and when it was all over, he would deliver a murderous glare which threatened nuclear retaliation once the opportunity presented itself.

And yet, despite all that, I loved him.

All this ran through my mind as I made my slow way home, and by the time I turned the car into the drive, I was near to tears. How could anyone be so cruel? How could anyone do this to me for no other reason than (illegal) financial gain?

There's nothing special about me. Like anyone else, I have my failings, but I don't number self-pity amongst them. I was not prone to sitting around feeling sorry for myself. On those occasions where I might legitimately indulge in such pointlessness, I used it in order to build my drive, my determination. Could I do so now? That was the question I asked myself as I walked into the kitchen and switched on the kettle.

And the answer was no. I could fire myself up. That wouldn't be a problem. But where would it get me? This person, whoever he or she was, was making demands, but as matters stood, there was no indication of where and when payment would be made, where and when I would collect my cat. Whatever drive, whatever anger, whatever sheer bloody mindedness I could generate would be useless.

What, then, could I do?

The sad answer to that was, 'nothing'.

I was still brooding on the prospect when Dennis came home from work. One look at me and he knew there was something wrong. "What's up, lass?"

"Cappy the Cat," I said as I prepared a beaker of tea for him. "Someone's kidnapped him, Dennis, and they're demanding a ransom. A thousand pounds."

He burst out laughing. "A grand? For that scabby little scrote? You're taking the mick, aren't you?" He looked around. "Where is he, anyway? At the vet's?"

"You're not listening, Dennis. I've been getting crazy text messages all day. Someone has kidnapped him and they want a thousand pounds or we'll never see him again."

The severity with which I told him the tale caused the truth to dawn upon him. "You mean it, don't you?"

"Of course I flaming well mean it." In a furious flurry, I opened the text messages on my smartphone and slammed it down on the table so he could read them. "See for yourself."

I watched his face screw up as he read the messages. His next announcement was inevitable. "It's tripe. It reads like one of Grimy's electrical repair reports on account of he can't spell neither."

"They're anagrams, Dennis, and when you sort them out, they tell us Cappy the Cat has been nabbed and they're demanding a ransom for him."

"Well, they've had it, haven't they? No way are we paying to get that little toe rag back."

Even without meaning it, my husband knew how to hurt me. "I want him back, Dennis. He's our cat. I love him and he loves us."

He snorted. "Gerraway. He's a vicious little swine. Always has been. He treats this place as if he owns it, and as for a support pet, he don't have a friendly bone in his body."

"He loves us all in his own way," I argued.

"No he doesn't. He's the same with everyone. He'd claw your eyes soon as look at you."

"He's very tender with Bethany."

"Which just goes to show about smart he is. He wouldn't dare do anything against her because he knows what you'd do to him."

I'd heard enough of this. "You don't know what this is doing to me, Dennis. Twice, maybe three times today, I've seen people who can't possibly be there. Petra Leach and Nate Kalinsky."

He frowned. "Bleach and Kaminski? You helped

send both of them down."

"I know. And they both got life. Yet, I've seen them both in Haxford today."

"You're losing your marbles, you are."

"No. I'm not. It's Cappy the Cat. I want him home, Dennis. No arguments. I want that cat back in this house before Christmas."

I'll say this for my old man. He always knows when he's beaten. He shrugged. "So what are you gonna do?"

My voice was reduced to a hiss. I may have been speaking to Dennis but I wasn't looking at him. "I'll wait, bide my time. Whoever this person is he'll need to meet with me if he wants the money. And then I'll have him."

Dennis put down his cup. "Sounds to me as if you've already made up your mind about who it is."

A vision of Norman Rushcroft came into my head. "I have. And when I come face to face with him, I'll make him regret every crazy word he's sent to me."

* * *

After such an exhausting day on Thursday, it would have been understandable if I'd been awake half the night, but notwithstanding my concern for Cappy the Cat, I slept well, and no, I didn't cry myself to sleep, even though I could have been excused for doing so.

The tweet of the mobile woke me at just after eight on Friday morning. An incoming text message.

In the space of less than twenty-four hours I'd

reached a point where I was reluctant, almost afraid to open texts, never mind read them. Cappy the Cat didn't like them either. With Dennis already at work, our moody moggie would normally install himself at the foot of the bed, and whenever the phone chirped, he would cast a look of utter disgust at me, as if to say, 'Can't you see I'm trying to sleep. Turn that stupid thing off'.

Cappy the Cat wasn't there. The pain of that thought pierced my heart like an arrow.

I reached to the beside cabinet, hovered between the phone and a glass of water, and I chose the latter in order to lubricate my vocal cords in case I needed to scream.

Thirst quenched, I picked up the phone, unlocked the screen and with a shaking finger opened the text app.

Relief flood through me. It was not from my nuisance messenger, but someone much closer and dearer to me.

Nan a, im txt yu on mams fone bethny

That darling child. Only four years of age and already learning to work with technology. She still had much to learn, obviously. Structure, spelling, the use of autocorrect and predictive text, but within the next few years, she would get there, and I foresaw the day when her fingers would dance over the onscreen keyboard like so many other youngsters.

I sent her a text back, saying, *You really are the cleverest little girl I know. Love, Nanna*, and with that done, I got out of bed and made for the shower.

It was while I was luxuriating under the hot

water that I heard the phone bleat again and Cappy the Cat temporarily pushed to the back of my mind, I smiled at the prospect of another message from my favourite child. I towelled off, and spirits soaring, hurried back to the bedroom to read her latest message.

Shock. That was the only word to describe the way my heart leapt. It wasn't from Bethany. It was my mystery texter.

Pan pitcher cries not getting the idea. Come brittle tar now 2k. June YOLO ex.

A few seconds earlier, I was elated, over the moon with my granddaughter's crude, infant skills. Now, I was all over the place. My pulse was up, my breathing accelerated, my thinking erratic.

I forced myself to calm down and racked my feverish brain, dredging up my police training for the difference between anxiety and panic. I knew there was a difference, but I couldn't remember what it was, and no matter how much I thought about it, that tiny gem of information would not come back to me.

I flopped on the bed, staring at the ceiling. Flouncing down on the mattress like that would always trigger a recognisable reaction from Cappy the Cat, usually a thunderous glare, after which he would jump off the bed, and pad away to the living room where he could sleep without the risk of being disturbed.

That sad thought alerted me to the difference between anxiety and panic. It was that word, 'trigger'. Anxiety had a trigger, panic was random, and needed no flashpoint. Panic was irrational fear, anxiety had an underlying cause.

With that realisation, I sat up, and began familiar, deep breathing exercises. Breathe in through the nose, count one, two, three, breathe out through pursed lips, count one, two, three, breathe in through the nose... and so on.

This, I decided, had gone far enough. I didn't care whether I had evidence or mere suspicion. If nothing else, these messages were nuisance communications, and the police were duty bound to take some kind of action.

I dressed, moved to the kitchen, snapped the kettle on with a good deal more force than was necessary, prepared a beaker with tea and sweeteners, and then moved to the table, where I sat and rang Mandy.

She and I had been friends for a long time, and she did me the courtesy of listening to me, but the outcome wasn't what I wanted to hear.

"I told you yesterday, Chrissy, I can't do anything. If you have time, bring the phone to the station, I'll get our tech guys to try and trace the source, but it'll be from a burner, and the best we'll be able to do is pinpoint the mast."

"I'll be with you in half an hour, and while I think on, warn Vic Hillman that you're expecting me. I've no patience for him and his temper this morning."

The kettle boiled, but I didn't bother with the tea. I was too frustrated, too angry, and all I wanted to do was get down to the police station and make a start on tracking the call. Instead, I gathered my winter wear, put on my coat, slipped my feet into fur-lined boots, left the house, and minutes later, I was on my way down the hill to Haxford.

I barely noticed the welter of Friday morning traffic. I was too focused on my missing cat and the outrageous demands of this mystery texter. Twenty minutes after leaving home, I marched into the police station ready to meet Vic Hillman head on, but it wasn't necessary. Mandy had told him and he ushered me through to her office.

She read through the three texts I'd received, and unofficially agreed with me. "I'd say you're right, but like yesterday, this garbage is too open to interpretation. You haven't seen anything of your cat since yesterday morning?"

"Not a peep. I've checked with my neighbours, I checked with Prenton's the vet, and I went along to see Bertha Ginsburgh. None of them owned up to seeing him. He's disappeared, Mandy, and I want him back, and it doesn't matter what you think, these texts are demanding money." I paused for a brief second. "And I have one person in mind. You seriously need to speak to him."

"He being?"

"Norman Rushcroft."

"And how come he's in the frame?"

I went into an explanation of my shaky theory, and when I was through, Mandy contemplated it for a short while before announcing her verdict. "I can see your point, but again, you've absolutely no proof. Have you called Ian with regard to this morning's text?"

"How could I? I came straight here after I rang you. But I'll bet you Dennis's quarterly divvy, that if I show Rushcroft this text, he'll crack it in a matter of minutes. As far as I'm concerned, Mandy, the only way he can get through anything this complex is because he composed it in the first place."

She left her seat. "Give me a few minutes. I'll get our guys onto tracing the source of the call." She gestured at her phone. "If you wanna ring Noiland at the Recorder, tell him to get Rushcroft down there, once we're ready, I'll come with you."

I agreed, and within fifteen minutes, we were sat with Ian – alone this time – waiting for his compiler to appear.

"He wasn't too pleased with you yesterday, Chrissy. Accusing him like that."

I dismissed the complaint. "You're mistaking me for someone who cares, Ian. He's cracking these idiotic messages too quickly for my liking."

"Because that's the kind of man he is. According to Lizzie, she told you how he rigged up an anagram of her name. I made the same bet with him, and he did it to me. My name's difficult because of the ten letters, five are vowels. Two a's, two i's, and an o. But he still did it. Anon laid in. When we checked it, it was spot on."

"With the best will in the world, Ian, I think I could have come up with that," I insisted. "But look at this morning's. Come brittle tar. Fourteen letters. It'll be interesting to see just how long it takes him to crack it."

"And have you cracked it?" he asked.

I shook my head. "The rest of it, yes, but that's easy. Pan pitcher cries is Christine Capper. June

YOLO ex was fairly simple too. The first message said *Feliz Navidad*, the Spanish for Merry Christmas. The second said *Buon Natale*, the Italian for Merry Christmas. On that basis, this one was easy enough to translate *Joyeux Noël*, the French for Merry Christmas. All that's left is come brittle tar. Let's see how fast he can crack it."

We didn't have long to wait. Within the next ten minutes, Rushcroft turned up, greeted Ian and Mandy, yet totally ignored me until I passed him my phone with the latest message.

He took out his notepad, wrote it out, and began to work on it. We remained silent, and I wondered just how that might affect him. I'd been in such situations myself and there's nothing worse than the pressure of expectant silence.

I wasn't particularly timing him, but according to my calculations it took less than five minutes.

"Not especially difficult when we consider the previous messages," he said. "It translates as terrible tomcat, and the full message reads, Christine Capper not getting the idea. Terrible tomcat now 2K. Merry Christmas."

I took my phone back and said nothing, but I laid a meaningful eye on Mandy.

"If you don't mind me saying, Mr Rushcroft," she rambled, "you solved that very quickly."

"I'm an expert, Sergeant. And as I said, we had the previous messages to go on. They all seem to be concerned with Mrs Capper's cat. Using that as a base, it wasn't really that difficult."

My favourite detective chewed her lip. "Do you own a couple of phones, sir?"

"Like many people these days, I own a smartphone, but that's all. And I have my landline at home, of course."

"Right now, Mr Rushcroft, I have my team tracking down the source of these messages. We can't track the number to an individual, which means it's what's known as a burner; an unregistered mobile phone. We can, however pinpoint the mast from which the signal was beamed. I wonder how close to your home the result will be."

Rushcroft was getting his dander up again. I could see it in his face. "You're accusing me, Sergeant? The way Mrs Capper accused me yesterday."

"No, sir, I'm not accusing you. I'm asking you outright. Are you sending these messages?"

"I am not."

"In that case, you won't have anything to worry about when we get our results, will you?"

"No, but you will when I instruct my lawyers."

Mandy actually laughed. "Since no one's accused you of anything, sir, you can talk to all the lawyers in the land. It won't make one bit of difference." She stood up. "You should be aware, however, that we take a dim view of people harassing others like Mrs Capper."

I felt as irritated with Mandy as I did with Rushcroft. I wanted her to take him in there and then. The long-ago police officer in me came to the fore. She couldn't do that. Not without grounds, and she wouldn't have any until she got the report from her tech people.

Something that had occurred to me before came back to me, and I challenged Rushcroft direct. "Does Trea Chapel mean anything to you?"

He looked blank. "Are we talking Methodist, Quaker, or what?"

"It's a name."

Now he shook his head. "Not one I've ever heard."

I snatched his pad and pen, wrote the name out in capitals and tossed them back to him. "Suppose it's an anagram?"

He looked down at the notepad, then up at me. "I'll work on it."

Chapter Eight

"That was a bit strong, Chrissy," Mandy said as we came out onto the street for the walk back to the police station. "Accusing him of hassling Harold Aubrey."

"It occurred to me yesterday," I explained, "After I first suspected him. The name you gave me, Trea Chapel, is so unusual that I guessed it might be an anagram. I challenged him on his knowledge of Aubrey, and he admitted that Aubrey had dealt with his mother's estate. Rushcroft's mother, that is."

"And did Aubrey make a cock and bottle of the job?"

"I shouldn't think so, but what price Aubrey acted for Rushcroft in some other instance?"

"You haven't asked Aubrey?"

"Not yet." I took out my phone. "But I will any minute now."

We'd reached the bypass where Mandy would cross the road to the police station, but she waited to hear what I would tell her.

I hit the recall for Aubrey's number. Jennifer Vetch answered and put me through.

"Ah, Mrs Capper. Delighted to hear from you? You have news?"

"I might have, but I need the answer to a question first. Have you acted on behalf of a man named Norman Rushcroft?"

The good cheer left him right away. "Oh dear." There was a pause. "I have, yes, but it's not something I'd care to discuss over the telephone, Mrs Capper, so if you're free, come along to my office now, and I'll bring you up to speed."

"I'll be with you in a few minutes," I assured him and cut the call. I beamed on Mandy. "I'm onto something."

"Keep me in the loop," she insisted. "Paddy's due down later this morning, so I might be difficult to catch, but make sure you let me know."

"Paddy? Something going down?" I asked. "Other than Trea Chapel, I mean?"

"Nope. Usual pre-Christmas call from him. Pep talk and a couple of beers in the CID room." She made ready to cross the road. "Ring me."

I gave her a thumbs up and turned back towards the crowded town centre streets. As on Thursday, Haxford was awash with people, all looking forward to the coming festive season, only now they were not alone. I was with them. I had my kitty kidnapper, I had my client's accuser, and I would enjoy Christmas. And Cappy the Cat would get an extra special treat from Santa. Dreamies by the hundredweight, a new, soft blanket for his bed, some toys, and best of all, Christmas cuddles from me... if he'd let me cuddle him.

When I got to Aubrey's office, Jennifer showed me straight through to his inner sanctum, where he invited me to sit, offered me tea, which I refused, and then instructed Jennifer not to disturb us.

He already had the file on his desk, but he waited until she had shut the door behind her before saying anything to me. "This matter, Mrs Capper, is confidential."

"Fair enough. Did it come to court?"

"Oh. Yes, of course it did."

"In that case, Mr Aubrey, as a practising lawyer, you shouldn't need me to tell you that it will be a matter of public record. I don't require all the gory details, but an overview of whatever happened will help me to help you pin down the person who has levelled these awful allegations against you."

It took a moment for my words to sink in. "You suspect that it's Norman Rushcroft?"

"I do. And the police have been informed of my suspicions, Mr Aubrey. Not that he may be seeking to slur your reputation, because obviously, I don't have any such information at the moment, but he's possibly involved in another case I'm working on. Pet abduction and a ransom demand."

He pursed his lips (why do lawyers do that) and delivered a long, slow nod of his head. "Quite the criminal mastermind, isn't he?"

"I haven't yet proved the case, Mr Aubrey. I'm hoping you can give me the lead I'm looking for." After my pointless preamble, I got us down to business. "I understand you dealt with his late mother's estate."

"Oh, that was simple enough. Only son, no other dependents, everything went to him, including the house. But I also acted on his behalf in a dispute with his next door neighbour."

Calm down, Chrissy, calm down. That's what I told myself, in an effort to suppress the rising excitement in me.

Aubrey went on, "About four years ago, Mr Rushcroft's neighbour put up a fence. He did so with the best of intentions. Mr Rushcroft had consistently complained about the man's dogs straying into the Rushcroft gardens. The neighbour – whose name I won't give you – did not consult Mr Rushcroft, who immediately complained that the fence was erected on his property, not the neighbour's. There was an argument, and one evening, Rushcroft tore the fence down. The neighbour demanded reparation, Rushcroft told him no, so the neighbour then sued Rushcroft for damages, and considering I'd processed his late mother's estate, he asked me to defend him." Aubrey sighed. "It was a long, and time-consuming process which involved the neighbour's lawyer getting in touch with the land registry to ascertain precisely where the fence was constructed. In the end, the matter came to court, and the neighbour's lawyer, a man you're familiar with…"

"My brother?"

"Yes. Your brother, Stephen, brought incontrovertible evidence to the proceedings that the fence had been constructed on the neighbour's property. In all such instances, the dividing can be thin, and in this case, we were talking a matter of less than six inches, but the argument was irrefutable. The fence was on the neighbour's property, not Rushcroft's. My client was instructed to pay damages amounting to the cost of replacing the fence. He was also ordered to pay the neighbour's legal fees, and over and above that he had my fees to pay. All up, it cost him a few thousand pounds."

It was all I needed, but I felt determined to press

for more. "And Rushcroft blamed you?"

"Well, if he did, he never said anything. He did ask me to follow-up your brother's research, but I told him there would be little point. I'd actually offered to do that research in the first place, before the case came to court, but Rushcroft declined. He was adamant that the fence was on his property. To do so after the hearing would cost him yet more money, and it was almost inevitable that I would come to the same conclusion as Stephen. Rushcroft left it at that. I've never heard from him since, and I assumed that he was... Not exactly happy, but reconciled to the court's decision. Now will you tell me why you believe he could be the one making these appalling accusations against me?"

I thought I'd already told him, but I went through it again for his benefit. "I'm receiving bizarre text messages indicating that my cat has been kidnapped, and the texter appears to be demanding a ransom. Whether you know it or not, Rushcroft works freelance for the Haxford Recorder, and the editor, Ian Noiland is a personal friend... of mine, not Rushcroft's. Ian engaged Rushcroft to analyse these cryptic messages. It seemed to me that Rushcroft got to the solutions too quickly and too easily. My conclusion is, he's sending them."

"Hmm. I have to say, madam, that Norman Rushcroft is highly skilled at constructing cryptic clues for crosswords."

"I'm aware of that, Mr Aubrey, but it does nothing to allay my suspicions."

He appeared bemused. "So what made you link your personal problems to the allegations made against me?"

"The name of your accuser. Trea Chapel. It's quite bizarre, and it occurred to me that it could be cryptic. I said at the outset, I don't know for sure, and the police are already involved in this matter. Once I speak to Sergeant Hiscoe, she'll bring Rushcroft in for questioning. If I'm right, your problem will be cleared up."

"And if you're not right?"

"Then I'm sorry, but we're back at square one." I stood up, preparing to leave. "I'll keep you informed, obviously. For the moment, would you mind if I had a word with your secretary?"

"Jennifer?" Aubrey was surprised.

"I believe she's the daughter of one of my husband's business partners. I'd just like a quick chat," I lied.

He acquiesced. "Please feel free to speak to her."

I thanked him, came out of the office, and collared Jennifer Vetch. After spending a moment or two speaking to her, I learned that she was indeed Greg Vetch's daughter, but she would not speak about her employer while we were in his office. Instead, she scrawled out her address, and invited, "If you come to my place after work, say about half past five, I'll talk to you then. But I'm telling you, I won't have much to say."

Haunted once more by suspicion, this time aimed at Aubrey, I agreed, came out into the cold once more, and the moment I was out of sight of both Aubrey's inner office, and Jennifer's outer domain, I rang Mandy, I gave her the overview of the things Aubrey had told me.

"Thanks, Chrissy. I'll get a couple of uniforms down to the Recorder, and bring Rushcroft in. If you wanna pop into the station later, I might have some news for you."

Not for the first time, I felt the pressure getting to me. In an effort to ease it, I put the phone in flight mode (it would keep pains in the BTM and nasty text messages at bay for a short while) then made my way into the market hall, and Terry's Tea Bar, where I ordered my standard toasted teacake and a cup of tea.

Despite the worry, I felt slightly encouraged. Instead of sitting round the house, moping, pining for Cappy the Cat and his errant ways, I had tackled the problem head on, given the police a lead they could follow up, a lead I was confident that would not only solve Aubrey's case but see the return of my pet, and hopefully send Rushcroft to prison where (as far as I was concerned) he belonged.

And Cappy the Cat's safety?

If I knew anything about Mandy (and I knew a lot) she wouldn't stop at questioning Rushcroft. She would arrange a search of his house and that would turn up my much-loved moggie.

As I sat there, revelling in a vision of reunion with my cat, Olivia ambled along the aisle, spotted me and hurried to join me.

"Hello, Mrs Lapper. Out shopping are you?"

"Trying to trace my missing cat," I told her and then realised it wasn't yet time for her to pick up the staff lunch orders. "What are you doing out of the studio at this hour?"

"There's not much to do, so I asked Dad if I

could go out and get some Christmas decorations for the place. I was thinking of some danglers and a jolly reef."

A jolly reef? It sounded like a spliff, but that wouldn't fit with Christmas, and when I thought about it, it wouldn't fit with Olivia either. As far as I knew, she was not and never had been into drugs.

"A jolly reef?"

"Yeah. You know. One of the reefs made of jolly with paper flowers and stuff on them. You hang them on the door and they say Merry Christmas."

The penny dropped. "You mean a holly wreath?"

"Isn't that what I said?"

I never got the chance to debate it with her as she switched the subject. "So Catty the Cap is still missing is he? I love him, you know. He's so sweet. When we used to record in your conversatory, he used to sit on my knee and he was as good as goals."

I remembered those times, and Cappy the Cat was anything but good. He was his usual tyrant self. He sat on Olivia's knee to the point where she couldn't move until he allowed it.

"Is it true that someone's stealen him?"

I nodded. "I believe so. He is missing, and I'm worried... and missing him."

"Tsk. How can people be so cruel? I'm sorry for you, Justine... Oh, while I remember, we had a phone call for you about ten minutes ago. Just before I came out."

I felt my heart rate go up. My worst fears were about to be realised. Someone had found Cappy the Cat dead. He'd been strangled. He'd been drowned.

He'd been cut up and dumped at the side of the road. And all because I tried to avoid paying the ransom. It didn't make a lot of sense. I hadn't even been told for sure that it was a ransom and I'd been given no instructions for payment.

That didn't alter my anxiety. The hall, the decorations, the Christmas saturation began to spin. On the stall next to Terry's, an ornamental Santa spun on his base, singing out, 'Ho-Ho-Ho', an echo of Reggie's Monk's fake ha-ha-ha, but Santa was laughing at me.

I was raving internally, my fury directed at the kidnapper and at the same time, turned inward upon myself. How could I be so mean? Was I getting like Dennis? Was my darling pet not worth the measly amount this evil person demanded? Where was this madman? In the custody of the Haxford police? Sat there, denying everything while laughing to himself at me?

I remembered the opening of the latest message. Christine Capper not getting the message. Well this certainly rammed it home with a vengeance.

Hold on… He or she had never rung before. It was always text messages.

Across the table, Olivia appeared slightly concerned. I dismissed it as part of her natural compassion. "A phone call?" I asked. "Not a text message?"

"No. Definitely a phone call. I took it. It was from somebody called Dam Me Kidney."

Dam Me Kidney? How could anyone have such a ridiculous name? They couldn't. It had to be another anagram. But with Rushcroft facing the police, who would I get to help crack it?

Then I remembered Olivia's irritating habit of getting names wrong. Good Lord, didn't she get mine wrong often enough? I spent a moment or two trying to work out who it might be, and eventually, I asked, "You don't mean Dan McKinley?"

"Hmm, yeah. Could be. I handed him over to Dad."

This was getting me nowhere. Dam Me Kidney or Dan McKinley, even Damn Mac Inlaid, I still didn't know anyone by that name. "So you don't know what this person wanted?"

"Well, initially he asked for you but I told him you weren't there because you don't work for us on Fridays unless you have an invertiew. Then he said he'd been to your house and you weren't there, so he asked where I might be able to find you and I didn't know, so I put him on to Dad, and he said exactly the same as me, excepting that Dad suggested he should keep trying your phone."

Odd then, that he'd been to my house but hadn't actually rung me direct. I didn't know who he was, why he wanted me or how he had found me, but no matter the source of his information, whether my website or my social media feeds, my number was easy to find. And what was he doing calling at my house? Clients didn't call unless and until I invited them.

Suspicion flooded my mind once again. Had this man turned up at my house carrying Cappy the Cat? Was he tired of waiting for me to respond to his idiotic texts, and had he decided to show himself in person?

If that was the case, how could it be Rushcroft? He was in police custody... Or was he?

My feverish imagination painted the scenario. Mandy and I confronted him at the Recorder offices, from where she returned to the station and I visited Harold Aubrey. When I came out of Aubrey's place, I rang her and she was about to get the wheels in motion. Would that gap, the time I spent with Aubrey, give our man time to grab Cappy the Cat, drive up to my house, find me AWOL, try ringing me (which he hadn't done) get in touch with Radio Haxford, and then... Do what?

Horror seeped through me. If I was right, then his most logical course of action would be to end Cappy the Cat's life, do away with the evidence.

I don't know how I stopped myself from bursting into tears, and across the table, Olivia realised my distress.

"Are you all right, Mrs Chatter?"

I pulled myself together. "I'll be fine, Olivia. You get back to whatever you were doing and don't worry about me."

I dug into my bag, took out my phone with the intention of ringing Mandy, and it was then that I realised why this mysterious man, Dan McKinley, aka Norman Rushcroft, hadn't rung me. He had. Twice. But I didn't know it because I'd put the phone in flight mode, and I can't comment on other people's phones, but mine didn't even register missed calls when it was silenced I that manner.

I cursed myself. Why did I put the phone in flight mode? To get away from the pressure for a minute or two? Was this what he'd driven me to? A woman so knotted, so tangled up with concern for her pet that she daren't even answer the phone, didn't even want to know whether people were ringing her?

I was going to ring him back. My finger hovered over the recall button, but I hung back and changed my mind. I rang Mandy instead. "Do you have Rushcroft in custody yet?"

"Get it right, Chrissy. We've brought him in, and we have him in an interview room for questioning. We'll decide on custody later. What's the problem?"

I explained to her what had happened in the ninety minutes or more since we left the Recorder offices. When I was through, she tutted.

"If you're right, he's covering his arse. I'll ring you later when we're through talking to him. If necessary, I'll get a warrant to search his place. It doesn't matter how clever he thinks he's been, he'll have left some trace of your madcap moggie."

If I thought I was distressed before, I was even worse now, and Olivia, who still hadn't moved, went to the counter to get me a cup of tea.

"My dad always says that tea's best for you when you're upset, Pristine," she said when she came back," and I'm not going to leave you until you're feeling a bit better."

I reached across the table and held a hand. "You're very sweet, Olivia, the kind of girl I'd like as my daughter. But you have work to do, and you can't stay here, babysitting an old weepy like me." I meant what I said. I wasn't just trying to get rid of her.

"Nobody cares at the studio, Justine. Half the time, they don't notice I'm missing." She tutted. "Until they want a cup of tea, that is. Then they can't shout me fast enough. I'll stay with you for a few minutes. Just make sure you're all right."

"Honestly, love, I'll be all…"

I trailed off as my phone (now out of flight mode obviously or I couldn't have rung Mandy.) tweeted to announce an incoming text, and unlike my angst first thing that morning and just now, I didn't mess about. I opened it right away and read with increasing fury.

Patchier princes, it's now £5000 for sue putty plans. Whine reach often.

Chapter Nine

That was it. The end of my tether. I just could not take any more. I burst into tears, head bowed, face buried in my hands, sobbing, weeping for my lost pet.

I was vaguely aware of Olivia rushing round the table, wrapping her arms around me, trying to comfort me, and then calling over to the counter, for Terry's assistance. I was even less aware of him leaving his other customers to his staff as he joined Olivia, sitting opposite me, taking hold of my hands, trying to encourage me to calm down, talk, but I couldn't do anything. All I could see was my poor cat in the hands of an evil tormentor who would (I had no doubt) have no hesitation in killing him.

I'm sure I heard Terry instruct Olivia to call her father, but I don't remember her making any such call. It was only when Eric came hurrying along the aisle to join us, that I began to slowly recover, take the tiniest control of my volatile emotions.

By now we were the centre of attention from Terry's customers, and other people who were passing the café. I didn't care about them. Let them look. If that's what it took to liven up their boring little lives, let them stare.

"She was all right until I told her about that fella what called the studio," I heard Olivia say. "Then later she spoke to Mrs Disco at the police station, and then she got a text and that's when she started crying."

Terry supplied more tea but it was the last thing I cared about. All I really wanted was my precious cat returned to me.

"What's going on, Chrissy?" Eric asked.

I was still too numb to explain properly, so I swept my finger across the phone screen, accessed the text, and showed it to him.

Puzzlement was his first reaction, soon followed by realisation. "This is like that silly message you received yesterday morning, isn't it?"

I nodded. "It's a ransom demand, Eric. The message yesterday was the start. This is the…" I couldn't think how many messages had already received. "It's either the third or fourth message I've received, and with each message, the price goes up."

"You're joking… No. I can see you're not joking. Olivia says you spoke to Mandy Hiscoe. I take it the police are involved?"

I nodded. "They have the prime suspect at the station. They're quizzing him now." The tears began to well in my eyes again. "If he's hurt my cat, I'll… I'll…" I trailed off. I didn't know what I would do.

"You're sure of your facts?"

"Do I have proof? No. But it's him. He's the only one smart enough to put together idiotic, stupid, cryptic nonsense like this."

Now Eric was at a loss for anything to say.

"It's cruel, this, Dad," Olivia said, and when I looked up, I could see she had tears in her eyes. "Pristine is the best we've got. She's always nice to me, and I don't understand how anybody could do this to her."

I took her hand. "Some people are like that, Olivia. This man is like that, and I don't understand why he should do this to me. Until I met him yesterday, I didn't even know him. What could I possibly have done to make him treat me like this?"

Eric was more rational. "You just said it. Some people are like that. You're well-known, Chrissy, at least in the Haxford area. He's seen an opportunity, and you often mention your cat, both on the radio and in your weekly vlog." His brow creased again. "I don't understand how he could have sent you this text message a few minutes ago, though, if he's in police custody."

I already had the answer. I don't know when it occurred to me. Probably while I was weeping, but it made absolute sense to me. "Remember the Allbrook business? Scheduling, Eric. He knew I was on to him. I made the mistake of challenging him yesterday, and Mandy and I confronted him earlier this morning. He probably guessed that they'd come for him, so he composed the text and scheduled it to be sent when he knew he would be in custody."

Eric nodded his understanding. It was thanks to his daughter, Olivia, that we had both learned that text messages could be scheduled for later delivery. "It sounds about right. Unfortunately, if he's being held by the police, how are you going to get your cat back?"

"Mandy assured me they'll search his place."

"If he's that clever, he won't have kept your cat there. I'm sorry, Chrissy. I'm not trying to make you feel any worse, but assuming you're right, he's a cocky so-and-so, and he'll have everything arranged so that the police will end up letting him go."

Once again, Eric's analysis made sense, and it was a symptom of my distress that I hadn't thought of that earlier.

The anger began to return. "They should let me at him. I'll put the fear of God into him. By the time I'm done with him, he'll be screaming to tell the truth."

I'd known Eric for a couple of years now, and his biggest asset was his decisiveness. "You're obviously a little calmer now. Does Mandy know about this latest text?" When I shook my head, he suggested, "Well, why don't you and I take a walk over to the police station and have a word with her. It might just be the piece of the puzzle that breaks this Rushcroft man."

Common sense once more. I agreed, got to my feet, and spent a moment at the counter, thanking Terry, wishing him the best for Christmas, and then while Olivia went about her errands, I accompanied Eric to the police station, a walk of about five or ten minutes through streets crowded with shoppers, a mass of people I envied. Their sole focus was Christmas, mine was a stolen, possibly frightened pet, held in a cage God knows where.

I noticed immediately that Vic Hillman was a good deal more cautious with Eric than he ever was with me. He told us that Mandy and Paddy Quinn were questioning Rushcroft, and would we like to wait. He would let them know we were there.

As it turned out, we didn't have long to wait, but it wasn't Mandy, and nor was it Paddy who came out to greet us. It was my son, Simon.

"Do you wanna come through, Mam? There's a bloke here who wants a word with you."

This was a mystery. Aside from the station crew, who else could want to see me? I didn't know anyone but Paddy, Mandy, Simon, Sonny Scott, Fliss Keele, and a few others.

Both Eric and I got to our feet, but Simon stopped Eric. "I'm sorry, Mr Reitman, but this bloke'll only speak to Mam."

The mystery deepened. I turned back to my producer. "Thanks, Eric. I'll be all right now. You get back to the studio, and if I don't see you before, I'll catch up with you on Tuesday morning for the agony aunt slot."

"You're sure you'll be all right?"

I smiled up at my son. "With Simon here, trust me, I'll be fine."

While Eric left, Simon led through to what I recognised as Mandy's small office, and that wasn't the only thing I recognised.

Sat behind the desk was a familiar face. I remembered him as being about six feet tall, looking trim and muscular in denims and brand-name trainers, sporting a short sleeved shirt which showed off his biceps. Now he was sat, the jacket of his expensive suit on the chair back, his white shirt reminding me of an advert for washing powder.

I hadn't been seeing ghosts. He was the real thing, but I didn't know which of the twins he was. Sparkling blue eyes and a pleasant smile played around his lips as he rose to greet me.

"Stop worrying, Christine. I'm Sam, not Nate."

Sam Kalinsky was a COSI – a Cabinet Office Specialist Investigator. Officially, neither he, nor his colleagues, nor even his department existed, and the last time we met, he persuaded me to accept what amounted to a generous financial offer in order to back off from a particular case. The alternative was he would ruin my reputation. Naturally, I toed the line. Not that I was too worried about my reputation, but at the time, Dennis was still very ill, and we needed the money.

Simon had left us, and I took a seat opposite Sam. There was a momentary pause, and I assumed that like me, Sam was wondering where to start, so I led. "I saw you yesterday. Not once but twice. Early in the afternoon on Vulcan Street, and then in the evening."

"You did indeed."

"I also noticed that you disappeared quite quickly. Where you worried that I was going to challenge you?"

"No. I wasn't watching you. I had my eye on a woman we both know, one you helped send to prison a couple of years ago."

"Petra Leach," I hissed. "I saw her too. She was outside Home Bargains, and later on, I saw her stood outside the library on Yorkshire Street."

"You're correct." Sam looked relaxed, totally at ease. "It was only when I came to the police station, earlier today that I learned of the problems you're having. As we speak, your friend, Sergeant Hiscoe, and her chief, Inspector Quinn, are questioning a man named Norman Rushcroft."

I nodded. "He's kidnapped my cat and he's demanding a ransom."

Sam laughed. "No, he hasn't, and he isn't."

I tutted. "Is this some kind of cover-up, like you did last time, because you and your department want words with Rushcroft?"

"A logical deduction, Christine, and were that the case, the department I work for would more than likely be the source of such suppression. However, it's not a cover-up. I don't know whether Rushcroft is at the root of your problems, but according to Sergeant Hiscoe, you've been receiving bizarre text messages of a cryptic nature, and I'm assured that Mr Rushcroft is an expert in such matters. I can, however, tell you that he is not the perpetrator."

I felt my confidence going. "For you to say that, you must know who it is."

"I do. Well, let me correct that. I have a strong suspicion as to who the perpetrator might be, and by now, you should have too."

The penny dropped, and everything began to come together, but it still didn't make any sense. "I thought she and her boyfriend were both sentenced to life."

"He's still behind bars, and he will be for a good many years yet, but she got the charge reduced to manslaughter on appeal. She's out now, on licence, having served over half her sentence. She was released about two months ago, and she's one angry lady."

"I can understand that, but she was guilty of a criminal offence. His activities came under the military which, obviously, is your business, but she was a police matter. How come you're watching her?"

"It's complicated. As you know, I sent him down for a good many years, but it's part of my brief to keep an eye on him. After a routine search of his cell recently, we came upon a contraband mobile phone."

"I thought it was illegal for prisoners to hold a mobile phone."

"Indeed it is, which is why I said it was a contraband phone. Because of the nature of his offences – and you know what they were – the phone came to me and I made an extensive examination of it. What I found were numerous text messages between him and Petra. Many of them were made while she was still in prison, from which I deduce that she, too, was in possession of an illegal mobile. That was confirmed when I found messages from her to him. Amongst those messages, Mrs Capper, were derogatory comments about you. I quote, I'll kill the bitch, I'll cut off her... Well, I won't use that kind of language because I know you disapprove, Christine, but it refers to your bosom. Later on, his messages advised against it on the grounds that she would go back to prison for life, and it would mean life. Instead, he recommended attacking you on another front, the kidnap of your granddaughter, Bethany."

I was horror-struck. I knew who he was talking about, and I knew how much she hated me before she was ever dragged back from southern Europe to this country to face charges. But to postulate kidnapping Bethany…

Sam interrupted my thoughts. "As it happened, she argued against it on the grounds that Bethany is the daughter of a police officer, your son, and that's when he recommended stealing your pet cat, and holding the animal to ransom."

I managed to maintain some control of myself and my feelings. "So you're telling me that she put the text messages together? I never thought she was that intelligent."

"Hiding her light under a bushel? I really can't say, but anything is possible. She'd been in prison for a couple of years, she may have taken advantage of some of the educational opportunities. On the other hand, perhaps she had a beef against Rushcroft, and coerced him into constructing the texts. I'm sure Sergeant Hiscoe and Inspector Quinn will advise you on that when they're done questioning Rushcroft. My concern, Chrissy, is for you. Believe it or not, despite my calling, which often demands total, emotional detachment, I understand the impact of pet abduction, and when your local police told me of your problems earlier today, I felt it necessary to come up here and give you the overview. Rushcroft may be involved, true, but he has not taken your cat. It's her."

Sam stood up, collected his jacket, and put it on.

We shook hands, and he then gave me the final warning. "If anyone should ask, this conversation never took place, and I was never in Haxford. I'll bid you good day, and please take my best wishes for Christmas." And with that, he walked out.

I never approved of twiddling my thumbs, so I

took out my phone, and rang Aubrey's office. There was something I wanted clearing up.

"Oh, hello, Mrs Capper. If you hold on I'll put you through—"

I cut Jenny off. "It's you I want to speak to, not your boss. The way things are, Jenny, I won't be able to get to see you at home, so let's deal with this matter over the phone. You must be aware of the allegations made against Mr Aubrey."

She was hesitant in answering. "Yes. I know about them."

"Well, Mr Aubrey insists he is innocent, the police believe that the person accusing him doesn't really exist, but you are the man on the ground… Correction, the woman on the ground. Does Mr Aubrey have any kind of inclination to that kind of thing? You know what I mean. Harassing women?"

"As far as I'm aware, Mrs Capper, no. I've worked for him for the last four or five years, and he did ask me out for a drink once, but that was at Christmas time, and I refused. I don't think there was anything in it. Just a quick Christmas drink, but I turned him down. I'm in a relationship and I'm not interested in anyone else. But as far as I'm concerned, that's the be all and end all of it."

"Thank you, Jenny. You have a nice Christmas."

The information was hardly definitive but it was enough for me. Harold Aubrey was innocent of the allegations made against him. Then it occurred to me that I was the one who insisted Trea Chapel was a made up name. With Sam's information, could I rearrange the letters to make up the name…

Yes I could. In fact it took me less than two

minutes, and it only took that long because I was using the tiny screen on my smartphone.

I came out of Mandy's office, crossed the CID room, and had a brief word with Simon. He listened to me, asked me to wait in Mandy's office again, and made his way to the interview rooms.

Five minutes later, Mandy and Paddy joined me.

"You had a word with the tea cosy," Paddy said. I knew why he was so disparaging of Sam. Paddy didn't like higher-ups treading on his patch. "Are you any wiser?"

"Yes. I know who's behind it, and she is also behind the spurious allegation against Harold Aubrey."

I slid my phone across the desk, and let them see the solution to the anagram, Trea Chapel.

"I thought she was still inside," Mandy said.

"According to Sam the mystery man, she appealed, and got the charge reduced to manslaughter, and she's out on licence. And yes, Mandy, she's here in Haxford, and she's holding my cat to ransom."

Paddy reverted to type and came in guns blazing. "I can see what you're up to, Chrissy, but let's be clear about this. It's a police matter. It's up to us to find her."

"And you really think she's going to get in touch with you to tell you where the ransom drop has to be made? Dream on, Paddy. If she wants the money, she has to contact me at some point, tell me where to make the drop. I'll be there to meet her, and I will let you know." I checked with each of them to ensure the message had got through. "Can I ask, where are you up to with Rushcroft?"

Mandy shrugged. "He's still denying everything, Chrissy, but assuming you and the super-secret agent are right and Rushcroft is not part of the heist, that doesn't necessarily clear him of constructing the cryptic messages, and we're looking at his laptop as we speak. I mean, I never figured her as being that bright, so she had to have help."

"I agree." I focused on Paddy. "I know it goes against the grain, Paddy, but how about letting me have a go at Rushcroft?"

His response was as I expected. "In the mood you're in? I'm sorry, Chrissy, but I'd be worried for Rushcroft's safety."

I held up my hands as a gesture of surrender. "On my honour as a girl guide, I promise I will not lose it. Knowing what I know now, I can pressure him in ways that you wouldn't be allowed to. I might just crack him."

My assurance was part nonsense. I'd never been a girl guide, but Paddy acquiesced. "I'll give you five minutes with him."

Chapter Ten

Paddy remained in the observation room, while I followed Mandy into the interview room. As I looked over Mandy's shoulder, Rushcroft didn't appear worried when she stepped into the room ahead of me, but when she sat down and he saw me, his features paled.

I smiled. "Hello, Mr Rushcroft."

He rounded on Mandy. "I don't know what game you're playing, Ms Hiscoe, but I will say nothing while she is in the room."

I sat down alongside Mandy and my smile became more acid. "My mother always told me that she is the cat's mother, and talking of cats, I've had another text message. Would you like to read it and see what you can do with it?"

He began to flounder. "I, er, I have business here which I need to deal with before I can think of anything else, madam. I really can't—"

Sliding my phone across the table, I cut him off. "I'm sure it won't take you a minute, Mr Rushcroft. Please. Have a look at it."

He picked up the phone, read the message, and then passed it back to me. "Whine reach often would translate as *Frohe Weihnachten*. It's German and broadly speaking, it says Merry Christmas. It fits with the foreign language greetings of the previous messages."

"And what about 'sue putty plans'?" I asked.

"I, er, I'd need time to analyse that, and right now, I really don't have the—"

For the second time, I cut him off, and I came in

hard. "You're lying, Rushcroft. I know who's sending these messages, and she doesn't have the brains to put this nonsense together. She needed someone to do it for her, and you are that someone. Now why don't you stop messing me and the police about, and tell us what's going on."

Judging by the look on his face, he'd never come across a woman so angry, a woman on the point of leaping over the table and beating him to a pulp.

"Sergeant, I must protest. This woman is not a police officer, and she has no right to be here."

Mandy retained her casual air of 'not really interested'. "Inspector Quinn and I think differently, Mr Rushcroft. Mrs Capper is the target of this harassment, and when this matter comes to court, her views will be taken on board. Victim statement. The beak will take her feelings into account when deciding upon a sentence. As far as we're concerned, she has every right to challenge you because, I'll be honest about this, we also know the person behind it. We know her well, and we're certain that she'd need help putting these messages together. She is local to Haxford... Correction, she was local to Haxford, and it's practically certain that since she was released, she's come back here, and the only person in this area who could possibly put together these cryptic irritations is you. I'll also tell you, that we've searched your house and brought your laptop into the station for examination. It's probably locked up with a password, but that doesn't matter. Our tech boys will crack that, and if we find one trace of even one of these messages on there, you're sunk." She fell silent for a moment, giving him time to process a long-winded announcement. Then she pressed him. "Why not come clean about it now?"

It was his turn to remain silent and it went on for long minutes. I was about to launch another attack, when he finally spoke up.

"Sue putty plans is an anagram of petulant pussy, a phrase you, Mrs Capper, use quite often when talking about your pet."

That was enough for me. I'd been right all along. He did construct the messages.

Struggling to rein in my fire, I suggested, "Suppose you tell us the full story."

More silence while he thought about the prospect. He fixed Mandy's eyes with his gaze. "I want immunity from prosecution."

Mandy laughed. "Where do you think you are? Playing a part in some American detective series? We don't do deals but if you co-operate, that will be mentioned in court, should we actually come to pressing charges. Now do as Chrissy suggests, and tell us what it's all about."

Another brief interlude of total silence before he finally began to speak.

"The incident I'm going to talk about goes back... oh, about ten years. At the time, I was working as a reporter for a regional newspaper, based in Leeds. I didn't specialise in any particular area, but I was preparing a series on general banking in the West Yorkshire area. It involved speaking to senior managers within the banking industry at a number of institutions. I was approached by a couple of men, both obviously criminals. They'd been watching me, and they wanted inside information on a specific bank. How much money was held on the premises, what kind of security arrangements they had in place, possible silent alarm systems, you know the kind of thing I mean. They offered me a thousand pounds in cash, plus a bonus based on the amount they got away with if I could deliver the necessary information. At the time, I'd just come through an expensive divorce, I was living with my mother, and I was down on my uppers. They assured me that my involvement in this outrageous scheme would never be traced. As far as I was concerned, it was easy money, and if it went wrong, I was in a prime position to deny any accusations they might bring against me. Well, it didn't go wrong. A few days after I delivered the necessary information – which, by the way, was easy to come by – the bank was robbed. Worse, it was an armed robbery, and one of the security officers was shot, badly injured. According to reports, they got away with about four thousand pounds." A look of pleading came to his face. "I was terrified. I knew they were going to rob the place, but I didn't know they would be armed. I never received any further payments from them. In fact, I never heard from them again, and for my own sake, I lay low. I dreaded a call from the police. As it happened, they were never caught, and no one, not the police, not them, ever came to speak to me. After a while, I felt confident that I'd got away with it."

Once he stopped talking, Mandy jumped in. "Who were these people?"

"They never identified themselves, and I never knew who they were... until about two months ago, when a woman approached me. She called herself Rachel Peat. She was quite open and honest about her situation. She had just been released from prison, having served half her sentence for manslaughter. She had some kind of relationship with the man who used to own Jumping Jacks, a chap named Augustus Leach. She knew everything about that bank robbery, including my involvement, from which I deduced that some of Leach's people had carried it out. She made it plain that unless I did as she asked, she would go to the police with that information." Rushcroft begged again. "What could I do? I had to do as she asked."

"And her first demand was an anagram of her name," I said.

He nodded. "Not difficult, as I'm sure you've already worked out, Mrs Capper. She had a serious issue with you. Apparently, you were responsible for her going to prison."

"Rubbish," I said. "All I did was pass on information to the police."

"She doesn't see it in quite the same light. According to what she told me, you ruined her life, and she was determined to make you pay for it."

"So you did as she asked, constructed these ridiculous text messages, and sat back while she abducted my cat?"

He nodded again. "I daren't do any other. What I didn't expect was Noiland calling me in to analyse the text messages. And I have to say, I didn't expect you, Mrs Capper, to realise that I might have put them together."

"Where did Harold Aubrey fit into this?" Mandy asked.

Rushcroft shrugged. "All she told me was that Aubrey was the duty solicitor appointed to defend her when she was brought back to this country, to this town. He couldn't mitigate her offence, and he advised her to plead guilty. That only served to annoy her further. But most of her overwhelming anger was aimed at you, Mrs Capper."

I was beginning to lose it again. "Where is my cat?"

"I don't know. I'm sorry. She kept those kind of details to herself. My involvement was no more than constructing the messages you've received."

"Then how the hell am I supposed to pay her?"

"You will receive one more text message, probably later today, and it will tell you where and when to meet her."

Mandy sat forward. "The message content?"

He shrugged. "I don't know." He shrunk under my fiery glare. "Honestly, I do not know. All I can give you is the first line which I constructed, and it's in plain English, aside from the time, which is in Roman numerals. That line reads, MCM with 10k, be there or… And that's how it ends. Wherever it is, Mrs Capper, she didn't tell me, but you're expected to be there with the money at seven p.m."

"But she didn't tell you where? I don't believe you."

If it were possible, he would be on his knees. "Please, I'm begging you. That is all I know. If I knew where she wanted to meet you, I would tell you, but she didn't tell me."

At that point, Paddy came into the room, and asked me to leave. Mandy and Simon were detailed to take a formal statement while Paddy took me back to Mandy's office.

"You did well there, Chrissy, and you have my thanks, but that's as far as it goes for you. When you get this final message, *if* you get this final message, you get in touch with us, and we'll handle it from there."

"And you can guarantee that you'll get my cat back, can you?"

He shrugged. "All I can say is we'll do our best."

I could have argued with him, but I knew it would be pointless. Instead, I agreed, came out of the police station, made my way back to the market and sat in my car.

It was all very well Paddy saying they would do their best. I took that as a given. But he and his colleagues, one of whom was my son, couldn't guarantee that Cappy the Cat would be returned unharmed. Indeed, for all I knew, she might have already murdered my pet. Is murder the correct description when talking about the senseless slaughter of an animal? I wasn't that bothered about precise English terminology. He was my cat, and if she killed him, then, as far as I was concerned, it was murder.

On the other hand, I had little choice but to remain optimistic, wait for this final message, then go out to meet her. I would handle the confrontation – for that is what it would be – on spec, make my decisions, take whatever action was necessary when we came face to face.

I don't know how many times I've said in my life that I don't do confrontations, and I wasn't stupid enough to imagine that I could fight with this woman and beat her. I'd need help, but she would no doubt demand that I attend alone. How would I get round that?

Logic told me that much would depend on the rendezvous. It wouldn't be anywhere in town, it wouldn't be anywhere near my home, indeed, as I thought about it, the most likely place would be somewhere out on the moors. Could I possibly get someone to help me and yet remain hidden until he/she was needed?

Dennis was out. His idea of discretion was a big hammer. The same applied to his business partners. So who else?

That's when it struck me. The perfect person. I took out my phone and rang her.

"Where are you up to, Chrissy?" Lizzie demanded.

"I'm expecting a face-to-face with the cat-nabber later today. I could do with some secret support."

She chuckled. "As in someone your cat-nicker won't see until it's too late?"

"Correct. I'm on my way home. What say you meet me there in twenty minutes?"

She agreed, and I started the engine, pulled out of the car park, and made my steady way home.

Lizzie was there before me, and as I let us in I got this awful feeling of emptiness. It wasn't the first time. It had been with me since Cappy the Cat went missing a little over twenty-four hours previously.

Lizzie and I passed most of the afternoon in my kitchen and conservatory, discussing our plans, but they were little better than hazy ideas. We could not come to any firm decisions until we had a location, and that wouldn't come until the final message arrived.

In fact, it turned up at four o'clock, just as we were on our third cup of tea.

Hard fox river rose MCM with 10k. Be there or...
Ding dong dell, Cappy's in the well
Or he will be if you fail to shell
Locked in his cage
I deffo want my wage
And so we understand
The bill is now ten grand.
Smarmy Rex

It didn't scan very well, and I marked her down as a rubbish poet.

"Seven o'clock with ten grand in my pocket," I said to Lizzie. "Rushcroft told me that much. But where is hard fox river rose? And who is Smarmy Rex? It's not anything like her name."

She spent a few moments studying it. "Smarmy Rex isn't a signature. It's an anagram of Merry Xmas." She pronounced it as it was spelled, X-mas not Christmas.

"The rest of it can't be that difficult, Chrissy. At least, I don't think so. Hard fox has to be Haxford. As for river rose, it doesn't look that hard to translate. What kind of areas do we know where they could be described using those letters?"

I didn't even need to think about it. "Reservoir. She's talking about Haxford Reservoir." I fumed again. "She's threatening to drown Cappy the Cat."

Lizzie was delighted, but her elation soon faded. "Trouble is, it's a bloody big bit of water. Whereabouts?"

"There's only one way to find out. I think it's time I sent her a text rather than the other way round."

I spent a few moments putting it together and when we were both happy, I sent it off.

I know where you mean. Precisely where, was all I had to say.

I wasn't too surprised by the speed with which I got an answer, and this time it was in plain English.

Under the bridge. Alone. I see anyone else with you, and you can kiss your cat goodbye.

I showed it to Lizzie, and she was, once again, delighted. "You're not going to like this, Chrissy, but there's only one way we can deal with it. If we take your car, I'll duck down on the back seat as you get to the Waterside Inn. You get out, go on ahead of me, and I'll sneak out of the car while you're confronting her. At some point, she'll threaten to drop Cappy in the reservoir. The only way you will stop her, is to threaten her back."

I wasn't happy with the idea. "I don't do threats, Lizzie."

"Then like she said, you can kiss your moggy goodbye. For crying out loud, girl, there's no guarantee that even if you pay up, which you're not going to, that she'll let the cat go. You know what she's like. Hell, I didn't even know the woman, but

I knew about her reputation."

It was with some reluctance that I finally agreed. "All right. I'll play it by ear."

Chapter Eleven

Haxford Reservoir was in the heart of Wakey Moor, and the Waterside Inn stood near to the middle of the man-made lake.

As I turned off the main road and trundled along that narrow lane which would take us there, Lizzie climbed through the gap between the fronts seats, and lay low on the rear bench seat. Half a mile further on, I came to the Waterside Inn. During the spring and summer months, it was a popular watering hole. How they survived during the winter, I'll never know. A Friday evening, and even this close to Christmas there were only two or three other cars parked there.

As I walked away from the car and the pub I was carrying a small shopping bag packed with what might have been money. It wasn't, of course. It was wedges of newspaper Lizzie and I had prepared. There was a wall on both sides of the approach road. It was actually above a triple-arch bridge, the reservoir spreading out either side of it. I made my way to the end of the bridge, then down to the left, and sure enough she was there. Dressed in shabby jeans, tatty trainers, and a quilted jacket. In her left hand, the side closest to the reservoir's waters, she held a pet carrier.

Once upon a time, she had been a good-looking woman. Not in my league, of course, but then, who was? Somewhere in her early forties, she wore no makeup or jewellery, and according to my memory, she had lost weight during her time in prison. The smile across her small mouth was anything but welcoming, and her eyes blazed with... With what? Anger? No, not anger. Triumph.

I was trembling, nervous, but determined to mask it as best I could. "Petra Leach." My voice spat acid at her, but all I got in return was that vicious, superior smile. "I won't say I'm pleased to see you, but you should know that Rushcroft has told us everything,"

"He always was a worm."

I played for time. "I still don't understand why? What have I done to you?"

"You ruined me. You were so determined to poke your bloody nose in. You got me sent to prison, so I thought I'd give you a proper bloody nose." She eyed the bag. "Hand it over."

I ignored her demand and insisted, "I did as your husband paid me to do. And as I understand it, you were eventually sentenced for manslaughter, but that had nothing to do with me."

"You set the cops on me."

"I told them what I'd learned. Nothing more. It was up to them whatever steps they took afterwards."

Once more she indicated the bag with a nod. "Hand it over."

There was going to be no reasoning with her. Reluctant as I felt, I would have to go for Lizzie's plan.

I glanced at the pet carrier and Cappy the Cat lounging idly inside. Entirely typical of that cat. Not a care in the world, didn't have the foggiest what was about to happen to him. But he did lay a gimlet, resentful eye on me as if asking, "Where have you been for the last two days? You're my servant. You're supposed to protect me from bananas like this."

Petra spotted my gaze and nodded at the cage. "Weighted down with a couple of house bricks." She raised it high enough for me to see the bricks taped to the underside of the pet carrier. As she did so, I noticed the scratch marks on the back her hand. Obviously, she'd tried handling him at some point and he had reacted as he always did. Good on you, Cappy the Cat, I thought.

Petra's demands intruded on my thoughts. "Hand over the money or your precious Cappy the swine goes for a dip… without an aqualung."

This was the big test. If I was honest with myself, I didn't want to do it, but Lizzie had called it right and Petra was leaving me no choice.

"Hear me out first," I said. "If you drop that pet carrier in the reservoir, you won't see the money. In fact you won't see anything ever again, because I will duck your head under the same water and hold you there until you drown. Take your pick. Either put Cappy the Cat down on the ground or you die with him."

She laughed. "You seriously think you're big enough or tough enough?"

I shrugged. "Maybe. Maybe not."

At that point, Lizzie, who must have crawled out of the car after me and had been waiting by the corner of the bridge, emerged from her hiding place.

Her presence took Petra by surprise.

"But she's not on her own," Lizzie said. "I'm

here, and I'll be helping her, and between the two of us, we'll make sure you cark it. And when the cops ask, we'll swear that there was a tussle, causing you to fall in and you couldn't swim. And, of course, it's far too cold for us to risk our lives by jumping in to rescue you." Lizzie's smile faded and her voice hardened. "Put the cat down on the ground. Now."

For the first time, Petra showed some hint of... not exactly fear, but certainly concern. "You wouldn't dare. Neither of you."

Lizzie agreed. "On her own, Chrissy probably wouldn't, but she's angry about the way you've treated her pet and she has me helping her, and I'm not half as generous as her. You see, my dad drowned in this same water at the start of the year, and I'm still hurting from it. It was scum like you who put him in. They're nicely locked up, and if you use your loaf, you will be too. Put the cat down or you go for a dip with him and neither of you will come back."

The worry now turned to fear. "You ruined me," she screamed at me. "You and Aubrey. Every penny I had. Gone."

"Oh, it had nothing to do with you being a killer, then?" Lizzie asked.

"It was an accident," Petra screamed.

It seemed to me that Lizzie and I were like good cop, bad cop, with me playing the former. I kept my voice as even as I could. "You're taking it out on an innocent cat." There was something almost alien about describing Cappy the Cat as 'innocent'. "All because you're too much of a coward to face me?"

She denied it. "I'm not scared of you. I've never been scared of you. Not even when Gus sicked you onto me. I just wanted to bleed you dry, the same way the legal fees bled me."

"Well, you certainly caused me some worry, but it's over, Petra. Put Cappy the Cat down on the ground, and we'll give you a lift to the police station."

"Where we'll suggest locking you up with a solid water supply in case you still feel like life's not worth it." Lizzie chuckled at her (supposed) witticism.

Petra was beaten. I could see it in her face. She brought the pet carrier back in, away from the water, and I felt a flood relief.

And then a sudden, angry look of pure determination came to her face. "You want your precious puddy-tat… Take him."

To my surprise and no little horror, she gripped the pet carrier with both hands, and threw it at me.

My reaction was automatic. I held out my hands, ready to catch it, but when it slammed into me, the weight of the basket, the cat, and however many bricks she'd used to weigh it down, knocked me backwards and took the wind out of me. I tripped, fell back, the pet carrier dropped out of my hands, and rolled across the ground to a chorus of howls and spits from Cappy the Cat.

For a moment, I was panic stricken, fretting that it might roll into the water, but it didn't. It came to rest upside down, a couple of feet from me. Not that Cappy the Cat was upside down. He'd already righted himself, and was glowering at me, his eyes asking, 'what are you playing at, you stupid woman?'

Worried that the bricks might cave in the base of the basket, I turned it the right way up, and received another evil glare from my fiery feline as he had to get himself upright yet again. I swear that no matter what you did for that cat, he would never be satisfied.

A few yards from me, Lizzie had tackled Petra, and now they were scuffling, rolling all over the ground, lashing out at each other, and it was difficult to pick a winner. Abandoning Cappy the Cat for the moment, I hurried across, grabbed Petra by the wrist as she raised a clenched fist, and when she half rolled to tackle me, Lizzie grabbed her other wrist.

After a brief struggle, we pressed her face down to the ground and pinned her there, both of us gripping her wrists behind her back while she screamed abuse at us.

Lizzie was covered in muck, mud, and grime, and she had what looked like the beginnings of a black eye, similar to the one that I didn't give her the previous Christmas. At least this one was genuine, not the product of makeup.

Even so, Lizzie grinned at me. "What now? Shall we beat the crap out of her then chuck her in the reservoir anyway?"

It was tempting, but I disapproved. "Don't be silly. Can you hold her while I bell Mandy Hiscoe?"

Without further ado, Lizzie sat on Petra's back, pinning her hands beneath her broad bottom. I mean Petra's hands were pinned beneath Lizzie's broad bottom, not the other way round. The action brought forth another howl of foul-mouthed protest from the trapped woman.

My reported friend beamed triumph. "Bell the filth. She's not going anywhere."

* * *

With Petra handcuffed, pressed into the rear seat of a patrol car, Simon stood talking to Sonny Scott and Fliss Keele, and Mandy confronted Lizzie and me.

She made her feelings plain. "You should have called us, Chrissy, never mind taking her on face-to-face. Paddy ordered you to give us a shout."

I was more than equal to the argument. "What was it you told me the other day, Mandy? You couldn't take any action because the analysis of those cryptic notes was literally open to interpretation. Even after Rushcroft told us everything, you still couldn't do anything until that final message came in. If I'd left it to you, Cappy the Cat would be dead now. Either that, or I would be out of pocket to the tune of ten thousand pounds."

Mandy switched her attention to Lizzie. "And you. You've been warned before about taking arbitrary action."

"I was helping a friend," Lizzie replied.

I decided it was time I took a more positive approach. "Why not call this a citizen's arrest, Mandy, and then send her back to the nick for another five years for pet abduction... plus whatever was outstanding on her original sentence?"

Mandy tutted. "And how do we explain all the bruises?"

I strolled back, picked up the pet carrier from which Cappy the Cat was still watching. "She attacked us with a couple of house bricks."

"Attached to a pet carrier?"

Lizzie chipped in. "She threw it at Chrissy."

Mandy shook her head. "You'll get me hung, drawn, and quartered, the pair of you."

"You should take a positive view, Mandy," I said. "Not only have I got Cappy the Cat back, not only have I prevented her from extorting ten thousand pounds from me, I've also helped you clear up the nonsense allegations against Harold Aubrey."

A frown creased Mandy's blonde brow. "You're making a lot of work for me."

"It'll do you good." I glanced towards the patrol car and received a glower from Petra in return. "I imagine she had plenty of time on her hands when she was inside, and I'm guessing she used that time to plan this down to the last dot." I glanced at my watch, the face covered in grime. "It's pushing eight o'clock, and tomorrow is the last Saturday before Christmas. It's time I was getting home, settling my fine feline friend down, taking a shower, and getting ready for the week-long madhouse as from tomorrow. Can I pop into the station and make my statement in the morning?"

Mandy agreed. "Too right. We're on our way back there now. I'll get her cleaned up and walled up for the night, and I'll expect you first thing in the morning. And hey, if Paddy has anything to say, it's all your fault, not mine."

Epilogue

I cried again when I got home. Reaction. That's what it was. I released Cappy the Cat from his paltry prison, picked him up and cuddled him. And the rotten little so-and-so clawed the back of my hand. There's gratitude for you.

His bad mood didn't prevent him polishing off a full feed and several Dreamies, and nor did it prevent him sitting expectantly at the conservatory door, waiting to be let out.

"And don't disappear this time," I ordered him.

True to form, he ignored me, and ran out into the darkness. Needless to say, he was back inside five minutes. He never did like the cold.

There was no excusing what Petra did, but to be fair, Cappy the Cat looked healthy, so she must have ensured that he was fed and watered. Also, the interior of the carrier was clean, so she must have kept him in large cage or something. Somewhere where he had had room to attend to his toilet needs.

It was over and no one was happier about that than me. Cappy the Cat was back where he belonged, and even Dennis was pleased to see him when I got back from Haxford Reservoir. Not that our moody moggie cared whether Dennis was pleased or not. After another brief ablutions call on the Timmins' garden, he ambled into the front room, and when we checked, he was curled up on the corner of the settee, fast asleep and ignoring the both of us.

The next few days were lost in a flurry of

activity, preparing for the big C. Dennis tried to get out of doing his share by claiming he had to work on Saturday, and I allowed it, only to drag him out on Sunday for the annual mammoth shop in CutCost.

In the meantime, Petra was remanded in custody, and both Mandy and Paddy were confident that she would be on her way back to prison for a sizeable stretch come the New Year. Not that Paddy allowed Lizzie and I to get away with our vigilante action. We received a severe ticking off from him on the Monday morning, but it was tinged with gentle best wishes for Christmas and New Year, and that was the end of the entire affair as far as we were concerned.

Then suddenly, Christmas was upon us. Dennis and I spent Christmas Eve at Tony and Val Wharrier's party, then on Christmas Day, we had the family round, Simon, Naomi, and Bethany, and I spoke with Ingrid and Darren over Zoom. They looked well, they looked tanned, and if anyone wanted my opinion, they were enjoying life on the Costa Blanca.

On Boxing Day, we threw our major thrash, and it seemed to me that most of Haxford turned up, including Mandy and her daughter Darlene, Sonny Scott and Fliss Keele, who now appeared to be an 'item', Ian and Lizzie from the Recorder, and, of course, Eric, his wife Beryl, Olivia, and Reggie Monk, my colleagues at Radio Haxford.

A wonderful time was had by all, but Dennis pulled a fast one on the twenty-seventh, by going back to work, leaving me to clear up the mess. And

I do mean a mess. The house looked like it had been hit by Hurricane Hilda or whatever nickname the latest weather front had garnered.

The parties were repeated in other locations for the New Year, and on January 4, I received a Tenerife postcard from Hazel McQuarrie. She got home a good few days before the card arrived, and as I said to her, it would've been cheaper to pop it in her luggage and hand it to me over the fence.

Did I learn anything from the curious case of the captured cat?

Yes, I did. I learned that Cappy the Cat was more important to me than I'd ever been ready to admit. I also learned that I was a lot tougher than I'd ever believed, and finally, I learned that I didn't approve of the kind of vigilante action Lizzie and I had to take in order to secure the return of my cantankerous cat.

With the coming of the New Year, the world would have to take care not to cross Christine Capper, blogger and vlogger, radio presenter, private investigator and cat lover.

And that's it for now. It remains only for me to wish you all a Merry Christmas, and a Happy New Year. May all your hopes and dreams come to pass, and may all your pets enjoy the comfort, safety, and security of your home.

THE END

THANK YOU FOR READING. I HOPE YOU HAVE ENJOYED THIS BOOK. WOULD YOU BE KIND ENOUGH TO LEAVE A RATING OR REVIEW ON AMAZON?

The Author

David W Robinson retired from the rat race after the other rats objected to his participation, and he now lives with his long-suffering wife in sight of the Pennine Moors outside Manchester.

Best known as the creator of the light-hearted and ever-popular **Sanford 3rd Age Club Mysteries**, **Mrs Capper's Casebooks** and in a similar vein the Spookies Paranormal Mysteries. He also produces darker, more psychological crime thrillers as in the **Feyer & Drake** thrillers and occasional standalone titles sometimes under the pen name **Robert Devine**

He, produces his own videos, and can frequently be heard grumbling against the world on Facebook at **https://www.facebook.com/dwrobinsonauthor** where you're more than welcome to follow him and his work.

He has a YouTube channel at **https://www.youtube.com/user/Dwrob96/videos**. For more information you can track him down at **www.dwrob.com** and if you want to sign up to my newsletter and pick up a **#FREE book or two**, you can find all the details at **https://dwrob.com/readers-club/**

All books by David W Robinson

Mrs Capper's Casebooks

Mrs Capper's Christmas
Death at the Wool Fair
Blackmail at the Ballot Box:
Exit Page Ten:
A Professional Dilemma
Murder at Christmas Manor
A Call to Murder
Death of Innocence
Death at the Diet Club
The Christmas Festival Murder
A Quizzical Drowning
Scarborough Not Fair
A Cryptic Christmas Cat-Nabbing

Mrs Capper's Christmas Specials

The Sanford 3rd Age Club Mysteries
The Filey Connection
The I-spy Murders
A Halloween Homicide
A Murder for Christmas
Murder at the Murder Mystery Weekend
My Deadly Valentine
The Chocolate Egg Murders
The Summer Wedding Murder
Costa del Murder
Christmas Crackers
Death in Distribution
A Theatrical Murder
Killing in the Family
Trial by Fire
Peril in Palmanova
The Squire's Lodge Murders
Murder on the Treasure Hunt
A Cornish Killing
Merry Murders Everyone
A Tangle in Tenerife
Tis the Season to be Murdered
Confusion in Cleethorpes
Murder on the Movie Set:
A Deadly Twixmas
Naked Murder
Murder at the Christmas Meddlercon

Special Editions
Tales from the Lazy Luncheonette Casebook
Boxed Set #1
The Sanford 3rd Age Club Christmas Specials

The Midthorpe Mysteries
A case of Missing on Midthorpe
A case of Bloodshed in Benidorm

SPOOKIES Paranormal Mysteries
The Haunting of Melmerby Manor
The Man in Black

Feyer & Drake
(Published by Bloodhound Books)
The Anagramist
The Frame

LOOKING FOR A COUPLE OF FREEBIES?

Then why not sign up to my newsletter. I guarantee you will not be spammed and I'm not in the business of selling email address. You'll receive not more than two or three emails per month, but best of all when you sign up to, you'll be guided to a page where you can download not one but TWO FREE BOOKS.

Visit https://dwrob.com/readers-club/ for details.

Do you want to know where I'm up at any given time? Then why not follow me on Facebook?

You have the following options. Follow me on my Facebook author page or you can join reader groups at David W Robinson & Readers and Ex DSK Crime Writers or you can do all three.

I welcome comments and feedback on both Amazon and Facebook.

Go on. You know you want to.

Printed in Great Britain
by Amazon